LEGACY OF A GUNFIGHTER

Following his release from prison, all gunfighter Luke Nicholls wants is revenge against William Grant, the man who almost killed him. Unfortunately, when the two meet, things don't go as planned. Struck down by a mysterious malady, his confidence is shaken. More complications arise when a woman out to avenge the murder of her husband tries to enlist his help. He refuses, determined not to lose sight of his own ambition — but Grant has other ideas. Dragged into a fight for survival, the odds are suddenly stacked even higher against Luke . . .

TERRY JAMES

LEGACY OF A GUNFIGHTER

Complete and Unabridged

LINFORD
Leicester

First published in Great Britain in 2017 by
Robert Hale
an imprint of The Crowood Press
Wiltshire

First Linford Edition
published 2020
by arrangement with
The Crowood Press
Wiltshire

A catalogue record for this book is available
from the British Library.

ISBN 978–1–4448–4595–2

Published by
Ulverscroft Limited
Anstey, Leicestershire

Set by Words & Graphics Ltd.
Anstey, Leicestershire
Printed and bound in Great Britain by
T. J. International Ltd., Padstow, Cornwall

This book is printed on acid-free paper

With thanks to all those writing friends who spur me on — you know who you are

Prologue

Luke Nicholls felt a tingle in the end of his fingers and a drop of sweat course down his temple. That and the thump of his heart were all he noticed as he turned on the drunken gunman who had followed him out of the saloon and called on him to draw. It was a tinhorn move, reminiscent of a dime novel tale, but nothing less than Luke would have expected. Young and cocky, dressed like a dude, his hair neatly barbered, the kid had been goading him all afternoon.

He called himself William Grant as though Luke should know who he was. But he didn't. And he didn't want to.

Standing with the edges of his coat pushed back, the flicker of a kerosene lantern reflecting off his silver-plated ivory-handled Colts, the would-be gunslinger pushed back the brim of his derby hat and raised his voice, as much

1

to draw a crowd as for Luke's benefit.

'William Grant, that's my name. You won't forget it. I've killed seven men,' he boasted, drawing a small group out of the saloon and on to the plank walk. 'I'm so fast, my gun will be back in its holster before he has even drawn his.'

He stared at Luke, his eyes wide with unbridled excitement above the smirk on his fat-lipped mouth. 'Do you want me to use my left hand to make it fair?'

Luke remained impassive. He knew what the kid's game was. Get him riled. Force him to make a mistake. But this wasn't Luke's first fight either. Not that it mattered. Men like them were all living on borrowed time. Even this punchy kid.

Especially the kid.

Tick. Tick. Tick. The march of time.

As the clock above the white-painted church struck six, Luke dodged into a run as he grabbed for his gun and started firing. For a second it surprised the kid, but soon the roar of Colt versus Schofield shattered the peace and

2

gunsmoke filled the air.

As the hammer clicked on an empty chamber Luke wasn't sure if he had been hit. Then the pain hit him. It felt like a stick of dynamite exploding inside his shirt. He staggered, not so much from the impact, but more from the shock and his legs giving way. At twenty-four years of age, with a string of gunfights under his belt, this was the first time he had ever thought about dying.

As the smoke cleared, onlookers exploded into action. Men ran forward, grabbed Grant by the arms and took his guns. As they marched him away, he was still grinning.

Luke lay on the hard-packed and rutted ground, unable to move as waves of tingling surged through his body. He struggled to breathe as his left lung began to squeeze, forcing short painful breaths. His vision started to white out, erasing the faces that stared down at him not with compassion but with anger.

Then he passed out.

★ ★ ★

When he woke he was lying on a table in a darkened room. He wondered if he was dead, but he could feel warm blood trickling over his skin and a burning sensation beneath a bloody patch that covered the upper right area of his chest. At least there wasn't much pain now.

He tried to call out.

That was when it hit him. Crushing pain, like a safe being dropped on to his chest, made it impossible for him to breathe and he passed out again.

'How long since it happened?' someone asked.

Luke opened his eyes. A lamp flickered near his face, dazzling him as he tried to focus. Someone leaned over him: an old man with a streak of blood in his hair and spectacles perched on the end of his nose.

'I'm not talking to you,' the old man said, not unkindly. 'You just rest easy. I'm Doctor Bartlett and I'm going to fix you up.'

'You make sure he lives, Doc,' someone else said. 'Son of a bitch is going to stand trial for murder and I want him healthy when he hangs.'

1

Four years later

Luke Nicholls dropped his hand to the butt of the Smith & Wesson Schofield .45 revolver holstered at his waist.

'Whenever you're ready, Marshal.'

The sound of smashing glass and rapid gunfire sounded almost simultaneously across the lonely sundrenched prairie. As the echoes subsided, he broke open the Schofield, tipped out the spent shells, then thumbed fresh cartridges into the chambers.

'Reminds me of old times,' the marshal said. 'Me throwing bottles into the air and you breaking 'em. Damn, you're fast!'

'It ain't my speed I'm worried about.'

Luke picked out an empty peach can from the flour sack lying on the ground at his feet. He swung it into the air and

6

emptied the fresh load into it. The can danced like a kite caught on the wind. Keeping the gun in his left hand, he broke it open and emptied out the spent casings in one fluid movement. This time he only loaded five rounds before sliding it into the holster.

'It's getting late,' he said, walking towards the piebald mare that he had picketed near by. 'Let's get back to town. I don't want to miss the stage getting in.'

The marshal mounted his grey and joined him. Side by side, dressed alike in jeans, blue shirts and tan vests, they could have been mistaken for brothers. In reality, Dan Keen and Luke Nicholls couldn't be more different. A lawman and an ex-convict. Best of friends despite their differences.

'Do you reckon he'll be on the stage today?' Dan asked as they started off at a walk.

'If not this one, then the one after or the one after that. Only thing I know for sure is, I'm going to be waiting when he steps down.'

Dan frowned. 'We've been friends a long time, Luke, so you know I mean well with what I say next. Why don't you just keep moving?'

Luke didn't take offence. He had thought about it himself often enough.

'He'd catch up with me sooner or later,' he said with stoicism. 'I already lost the best part of four years of my life, I don't intend to spend the next however-long running.'

'Did you ever think of just changing your name?'

'I could, but I won't.' Luke eyed his friend sideways, a rare grin tickling his lips. 'What kind of a lawman are you anyway, suggesting such a thing?'

'I'm your friend and, while we chose different paths, I know you're not a bad man.'

Luke's mood darkened. 'Tell that to the family of the woman I killed.'

They picked up the pace and rode in silence. After being cooped up in prison for so long, fresh air and freedom were a luxury Luke didn't take for granted; and despite the brooding silence, he was determined to enjoy the ride.

The clock above the bank was striking four when they reached the outskirts of town and parted company. It was Luke's idea not to be seen together, although Dan had argued fervently many times that it wasn't necessary for them to hide their friendship.

You're the law and I'm a convicted killer, Luke told him time and again. You don't want that stink attaching itself to you.

★ ★ ★

After leaving his horse at the livery stable, Luke went back to his small room at the rear of the low-rent hotel where he worked as a night clerk. His accommodation was just an old storage cupboard really, but it held a cot and a small chest of drawers, adequate for his needs. He changed out of his rough clothes and into a dark-grey suit, white shirt and string tie, all of which were hanging from a nail hammered into the wall. The revolver he returned to its holster on his belt before heading across to the saloon.

'Howdy, Luke.'

'Jim,' he said, acknowledging the man behind the bar.

'Nice suit,' the barkeep opined, pouring him a glass of beer without waiting to be asked.

'All the way from New York.'

Looking into the mirror behind the bar, Luke surveyed the room. He didn't see anybody new amongst the dozen faces spread around, and no one paid any attention to him as he leaned against the bar sipping his drink.

'New York? Fancy that.' Jim looked impressed. 'I guess the cards have been treating you well lately.'

Luke chuckled. 'Better than the feller I won it off.'

Jim laughed and moved away, leaving Luke to sip his drink in peace. But although he presented a calm exterior, Luke's insides churned with anticipation. Feeling restless, he checked his pocket watch, then finished his drink and walked outside to lean against the empty hitch rail.

Ten minutes felt like an hour as he waited. When the Concord stagecoach eventually arrived and stopped outside the Grand Hotel, his nerves were jangling. He licked his lips, craving another drink as he watched the driver climb on top and start sorting through the luggage. It was another minute before the door swung open and the passengers started to disembark.

A portly woman and a small child were the first to step down, then a drummer clutching a battered case against his stomach, then a woman wearing a smart beige two-piece and a fancy little hat over neatly styled chestnut-coloured hair.

Luke kept his focus on the stage but no one else appeared. The driver tossed down the luggage to the shotgun rider, who had already descended from his perch. After they collected their belongings, the passengers moved away and the company men went into the hotel while the local liveryman swapped the horses.

Still Luke couldn't take his eyes from the stage with its door hanging open.

'Excuse me, sir.'

Startled, he looked down at the woman whose hand rested gently on his arm. She was at least a head shorter than he, but he straightened his stance to ensure that his view of the stage remained unhindered as he attempted to step aside.

She declined to pass, instead standing squarely in front of him.

'I was just wondering if you could recommend a hotel, nothing too fancy.'

It seemed strange that, of all the people on the street, she should speak to him. He knew the image he presented, with his fancy suit, polished boots and the Schofield outlined by a bulge inside his coat. He wasn't the kind of man a decent woman would choose to pass close to, let alone engage in conversation.

He glanced at her and recognized her as the woman who had got down from the stage. Close to, her beige-and-brown checked jacket looked a little faded, the neck of her blouse slightly frayed. Her face was tanned and pretty, and her blue-green eyes sparkled as she looked up at him, her easy smile hinting at a sense of humour. His gaze cut back to the Concord.

'There's the Beaumont down the street and on the left. It's small but clean. They change the sheets between customers.'

'Thank you. Who shall I say sent me?'

'It makes no never mind. Just ask for a room and they'll give you one.'

'I see. Well, my name's Kate Portillo, if you'd care to know it.'

'Pleased to meet you, I'm sure,' he said, without any genuine interest.

'And you are . . . ?' she asked, when

the silence between them lengthened.

He turned a scowl on her. 'Look, lady, you asked me for the name of a hotel and I gave you one. What is it exactly that you want from me that you need my name to get it?'

She seemed unruffled by his surliness, her smile widening to reveal clean, straight teeth and a single dimple in one cheek. 'I'm a stranger in town, a woman on her own. It's always good to have a friend, don't you think?'

'And I look like the kind of man you'd want as a friend?'

She looked him up and down.

'Why not? You're standing outside a saloon in the middle of the afternoon, wearing an expensive suit and carrying a gun that suggests you know how to handle yourself.'

Her blunt assessment took him aback. 'And that's a good thing?'

She shrugged. 'I guess that depends on what kind of woman I am.'

With the buttons on her blouse undone down to her perspiring cleavage, he guessed she was no preacher's daughter. Maybe at another time she might have intrigued him. Right now, she was a distraction he could do without.

'Whatever you're selling, I'm not interested,' he said, declining further speculation.

'Jeez, you're prickly. Can't a girl be friendly?'

She pressed a handkerchief to her nose and inhaled its scent as if it would give her the strength to deal with him. He caught a whiff of pine and flowers — maybe even camphor. For a split second it brought a flash of memory, but his temper was starting to fray and he had no patience with the intrusion.

'Look, what do you want?' he asked, punctuating each word.

'How about we start with your name and go from there?'

'If it'll get rid of you, it's — '

He brushed her aside and leaned forward, scrutinizing the Concord as it rocked slightly.

'You were about to tell me your

name,' she persisted, touching his arm more firmly.

He shook her off, his pulse quickening as a blond-haired man in a brown suit and derby hat stepped down on to the plank walk. He was thinner than Luke remembered, older-looking in a worldly way, but there was no mistaking him. Despite his diminutive height, his square shoulders tapering to narrow hips still presented a tempting target.

William Grant saw him and smiled coldly.

Despite people going about their daily business, moving between them without suspecting what was to come, it could have been just the two of them alone on the street. From fifty yards, Luke saw him as clearly as if they stood toe to toe.

Kate shook his arm, talking at him. Again he smelled the scent that wafted from her handkerchief. He noticed his heartbeat seeming to fight against his chest, deafening him like a hammer pounding rocks inside his head. His fingers tingled. His palms itched with the same sweat that broke out all over his body.

He looked down into Kate's face, but her features were unclear as they swam before his eyes. For a split second, he saw another face and his heart seemed to stop. He grabbed at his chest.

'What's wrong?' Kate asked.

A wave of nausea passed over him. It left him feeling light-headed and dizzy. If he didn't sit down soon his legs were going to give out. Already his vision was starting to lose detail.

He staggered and Kate caught his weight across her shoulders, almost buckling under him but, despite appearances, she was a strong little thing. And she needed to be as he felt the strength draining from him.

'My name's Luke Nicholls,' he blurted through gasps as he clutched his chest. 'Help me to the Beaumont and we'll go from there.'

2

Kate struggled to keep her feet as they staggered to the hotel. It wasn't far but her back felt ready to break by the time they crashed through the front doors. Although Luke was lean, his incapacity made him little less than a dead weight.

The lobby was empty and there was no one at the front desk when they entered.

'Where's your room?' she asked.

Luke pointed off towards the back and pushed her along until they reached a door, where he fell against the wall.

'The key's in my pocket,' he managed between gasps.

After a quick fumble around, she found it and unlocked the narrow door, putting her shoulder against the flimsy panel when it wouldn't open.

'Pull,' he instructed.

It opened easily then, and she peered inside at the small windowless space; it was barely big enough to contain him, let alone both of them.

'You're not stopping here,' she said, shaking her head as she slammed the door.

Before he could argue, she yanked his arm and dragged him back to the lobby, almost knocking over the clerk, who was carrying a cup of coffee in one hand and a plate of sandwiches in the other.

'What the . . . ?' He didn't look at them as he concentrated on keeping his grip on the food.

'I need a room,' Kate said. 'Give me a key.'

'I can't just give you a key.' The clerk settled his coffee on the desk, bending over to wipe a splash of liquid from the leg of his pants.

'Would you sooner have your guests stepping over a man lying dead in the middle of the floor?'

Still the clerk didn't look at them.

'What's wrong with him?'

'I don't know. Heart maybe. The sooner we get him into bed and fetch a doctor the sooner we'll know.'

'Well, I don't ... ' he whined. 'It's — '

'Jeez, Orville! Just give her a key,' Luke mustered the breath to utter.

At last the young, oil-haired, bespectacled clerk gave them his attention.

'Luke?' he said, startled. 'What happened? Are you all right?'

'Key,' they shouted together.

Orville grabbed one from the board behind the desk, then pushed the register towards Kate. It cost her an effort not to unleash her frustration on him, but instead of voicing the string of unladylike invectives that sprang to mind, she snatched the key.

'Where's the room?' she demanded.

Looking embarrassed, Orville snapped the book shut.

'U . . . up the stairs and on the left.' He started to come round the desk. 'Let me give you a hand with him.'

'No!' Her tone brooked no argument. 'You fetch a doctor. Tell him it might be life or death.'

When the clerk didn't immediately move, she glared at him. '*Now*, please.'

★　★　★

The room had seen better days, but it was large and well furnished with a big bed, on to which Kate shoved Luke before loosening his collar and removing his boots and belt. By the time the doctor arrived twenty minutes later, she was sitting on a ladder-back chair by the window, sipping coffee out of a china cup while Luke sprawled listlessly on the bed with his eyes closed. His breathing was returning to normal and he had stopped clutching his chest, but his face was pale as milk and he hadn't said another word.

Kate eyed the doctor with growing reservations. A wiry, middle-aged man with dull brown hair, red cheeks and bright blue eyes, his faded black suit looked as though he might have slept in it. That he liked his drink was apparent before Kate smelled the whiskey on his breath. As he made his examination, he alternately nodded and shook his head, mumbling as he listened to Luke's heart.

Feigning lack of interest at what was going on in the room, Kate looked out on to the street. In truth, her attention was split between the need to know if Grant had followed them and what was wrong with Luke Nicholls. That he wasn't quite the man she had expected was already apparent, but whether he would prove to be useful despite his shortcomings remained to be seen.

'What were you doing when it started?' the doctor asked Luke.

'Standing in the street talking to that lady over there.'

'And did she say anything that disturbed you?'

'No.'

'So nothing was said or happened

that might have caused you to become agitated?'

When Luke didn't immediately answer, Kate turned to look at him. As he stared back at her, the message was clear enough in his hard, steady gaze. *Say nothing.*

She nodded her understanding.

'Nothing,' Luke said.

Whether the doctor had seen what passed between them was impossible to say as he wound up his stethoscope and packed his bag.

'So, is it his heart?' she asked, when the silence stretched out.

'I don't believe so.'

Luke sighed as if he had been holding his breath.

'What caused me to feel like I was dying then, Doc?'

The medic eyed the gun lying in its holster at the foot of the bed. Chewing on his bottom lip, he looked reluctant to give his diagnosis.

'You might as well just come out with it,' Kate suggested, with a little laugh.

'You won't get paid until you do.'

The medic considered the trade-off, then shrugged. 'As far as I can tell, you're as fit as the proverbial fiddle, Mr Nicholls.'

'Then why did I feel like I was dying?'

'I'd say you suffered an attack brought on by' — he cleared his throat — 'anxiety.'

'Anxiety?'

'Something happened that caused you to be agitated, fearful maybe, and your mind overreacted, causing the symptoms you felt.'

Luke scowled. 'Will it happen again?'

'Hard to say. My advice would be to figure out what brought it on and try to avoid it in the future.'

Kate watched Luke's expression as he pondered the news. It didn't seem to surprise him, but neither did it please him, judging by his deepening scowl. He took a couple of coins from his pocket and offered them to the doctor.

'Thanks for coming over. Whilst I

don't put much faith in what you've said, I'd appreciate it if you kept it between us.'

The doctor took one of the coins and dropped it into his vest pocket. 'I never share patient information, Mr Nicholls,' he said, sternly, before heading for the door. 'If it happens again, I suggest you try to breathe easy and take a few minutes to collect yourself.'

After showing him out, Kate closed the door and stood with her back against it, watching Luke fasten his shirt with shaky fingers before he pulled on his boots. As if he felt her gaze on him, he looked up, his thoughts unreadable behind steady grey eyes. For a moment, he reminded her of her husband Frank, although physically they were nothing alike. Frank had been darkly handsome, broad-shouldered and larger than life. Luke was average at best and difficult to read.

'You must be thinking you made a mistake talking to me,' he said, buckling on his belt. 'Not quite what you were expecting, I'm sure.'

Snapping out of her daze, she chuckled, deciding not to give up on him just yet.

'How about you buy me dinner later and I'll be the judge of that?'

3

The hotel dining room filled up quickly in the evenings but the waiter, knowing Luke as a fellow employee of the Beaumont, had saved him a quiet table in a shadowy corner. Although it suited his needs, Luke guessed its location had more to do with keeping him away from the decent folk than affording him his privacy.

'What'll it be, Luke?' the waiter asked when he returned with their drinks.

'Steak and potatoes still on the menu, Bill?'

'You know it is,' he said, grinning. 'And for your lady friend?'

'I'll have the same,' she said before Luke could answer for her.

They sat in silence, Luke sipping whiskey and Kate sipping water, each looking at the other with interest. Luke imagined that her boldness might bother some men but she intrigued him with her air of worldliness and the hint of amusement that never left her blue-green eyes or the corners of her Cupid's bow mouth. With the blush of a hot, rose-scented bath still on her skin and wisps of damp hair curling around her face, she was a mighty attractive woman.

'So, how much of a scene do you think I caused?' he asked.

'I think your reputation is intact, if that's what you're worried about.'

He feigned ignorance at her meaning but, judging by the spontaneous guffaw she let out, he wasn't fooling her.

'I know what kind of man you are, Luke . . . do you mind if I call you Luke?'

He shrugged. He had been called worse.

'Half the men in this restaurant,' she continued, 'are too afraid to look in your direction and half the women are too curious not to.'

He glanced around the small room to

28

test her theory. Although Kate herself was garnering some attention, it was true that if he shouted *boo!* most of the men would run out, leaving their womenfolk to swoon unaided.

'And that doesn't bother you?'

Her laughter tinkled like a glass bell. 'You don't think it was a coincidence that I spoke to you in the street, do you?'

He'd had his doubts but curiosity wasn't one of his weaknesses so he merely shrugged. If she had a reason for singling him out, she'd tell him. In his experience women liked to talk.

Just then the food arrived and she leaned back slightly from the table as the waiter placed down the steaming plates.

'Looks good and I'm starving,' she said. 'Let's eat.'

Despite her diminutive frame, Kate Portillo took her food seriously and they ate in silence. When Bill brought out peach cobbler for dessert she made light work of it while Luke sipped coffee and watched the dining room empty as the other patrons finished eating and left.

At last Kate sat back and clasped her hands across her stomach.

'You enjoyed that,' Luke said, sliding a cup of coffee across to her.

'I did.' She added a generous amount of cream. 'It's been a while since a man bought me dinner. Thank you.'

Truth be told, he should be thanking her. It had been a while since he'd had company for dinner and she was a pleasant distraction.

'You're welcome,' he said, 'but I don't need to tell you it came with a price, do I?'

She looked him dead in the eye. 'Everything does, but I think I'm still in credit.'

'Are you?' he asked, feeling relaxed as her coquettishness and the brandy in his coffee lowered his defences. 'How about you tell me something about yourself and I'll be the judge of that?'

'There's not much to tell,' she said, concentrating on drinking her coffee. 'I'm a widow.'

'That's all I get?' he asked when nothing more was forthcoming.

A flicker of sadness flattened her smile, her eyes losing their glint of mischief for just a split second.

'My husband was a gambler. He bet against the wrong man,' she said simply. 'Now it's your turn. Tell me something about Luke Nicholls.'

He had been feeling relaxed and comfortable in her company. She was easy on the eye and her playful banter amused him, made him aware of the loneliness that dogged him, but he wasn't the kind of man she should keep company with. His reply was harsher than he intended.

'I'm trouble. That's all you really need to know about me. Not the marrying kind, if that's what you're looking for.'

'I've heard that before and it turned out to be true.' She chuckled. 'But if you think that's my intention you're mistaken.'

He stood and dropped a handful of money on to the table.

'Let's hope so, Mrs Portillo, because I'd hate for you to waste your time on a lost cause like me.'

She nodded but didn't try to stop him leaving.

He was glad about that.

4

'Sure, Luke's a regular,' Jim said, pouring a second shot of whiskey. 'You'll find him in here most afternoons and evenings.'

Grant faced the room and pressed his back up against the bar, resting his elbows on the scarred oak top as he looked around. Out of habit he assessed each of the half-dozen men drinking or playing cards at the few tables scattered around. Those who bothered to return his attention were careful not to catch his eye or stare at the ivory-handled Colts.

'I don't see him,' Grant said.

'You won't at this time.'

The news irritated him but Grant tried not to let it show. 'Why not?'

'He works as the night clerk over at the Beaumont. His shift starts at eleven o'clock. If he ain't in here by eight of an

33

evening, he ain't coming.'

Grant glanced at his pocket watch. It showed nine o'clock; he frowned.

'Looks like I'm in for a quiet night then. Best leave me the bottle and a deck of cards.'

'Don't think you'll find many players in here,' Jim said, placing both items on the bar. 'These boys'll be turning in soon and I'll be shutting up around midnight.'

'I didn't know places like this ever closed.'

'There's only me here and I need to sleep sometime. The town's quiet during the week so I close up early. Come the weekend, the doors'll be open all day and night.'

Jim moved away as another patron entered through the split doors. A cursory glance at the roughly clothed newcomer told Grant he was of no consequence. Glass, bottle and cards in hand, he found a table in the middle of the room and dealt himself a hand of solitaire.

★ ★ ★

Sitting behind the front desk of the Beaumont, Luke looked at his pocket watch. Ten after midnight. It seemed like hours since he had last checked the time but in reality it was no more than twenty minutes. Pushing back his chair, he stood and stretched before moving to the wall sconces and extinguishing lamps set around the lobby. He left those nearest the entrance burning on a low wick. There was little chance anyone would check in this late, but a weary traveller should still be able to find his way safely across the lobby. As for the hotel's current guests, a glance at the almost empty key rack told him that they were already in their rooms.

Noticing a single glove lying at the foot of the stairs, he scooped it up and placed it in the bottom drawer of the desk with several other lost and found items, including a single shoe that had been there for weeks. He shook his head every time he saw it. How did a man lose a shoe without noticing? A glove, a bandanna, a cufflink were understandable, but a shoe?

He closed the drawer and picked up his empty cup, eyeing it glumly. With a quick look around the lobby and up the stairs, he headed to the kitchen at the back of the building. There was a plate of leftovers on the table and a pot of coffee on the stove and, knowing they were for him, he carried them back to his desk along with an extra cup for Dan. The marshal was working the night shift so the chances were he would stop in during his rounds, and despite trying to keep him at a distance, Luke enjoyed Dan's company. His frequent letters had been Luke's only highlight when he was in prison.

'You're right on time,' he said, hearing the front door open and close and footsteps coming in to the lobby. 'Coffee's hot and there's a piece of peach cobbler here with your name on it.'

'I hate peaches.'

The tray rattled as Luke shoved it on to the desk. He looked up; his heartbeat quickening as he watched Grant idle towards him.

'You're not wasting any time then?' Luke asked, aware of the dryness inside his mouth.

'It's been four and a half years. I think I've been patient.'

Luke fanned his hands out to the side, willing them not to tremble.

'I'm not carrying a gun.'

'I can see that. You didn't turn yellow, did you?'

Luke bristled but without a gun he was helpless.

'It's hotel policy for employees not to be armed.' His answer was matter of fact. 'It upsets the guests.'

'That's all right then. I didn't come here to kill you tonight, anyway.'

The admission didn't make Luke any less tense.

'Then what do you want?'

'Don't get me wrong,' Grant said, showing a full set of good teeth in a disingenuous smile. 'I want to kill you.'

Luke hardly saw Grant's hand move before a Colt appeared in it. He realized he had gone for his own gun without thinking as his hand grasped at air.

'And I will kill you,' Grant said, twirling the gun before sliding it back into its holster. 'Just not here and not now. That would be too easy.'

Luke swallowed to moisten his mouth, but it didn't help.

'Well, unless you want a room,' he managed, clearing his throat, 'I'm going to have to ask you to leave.'

Grant's eyes narrowed, his thick lips moving into a strange pucker, but before he could say or do anything the street door opened and Dan Keen pushed inside carrying his Winchester rifle.

'It's starting to rain out there,' he said, his gaze moving between the two men as he brushed the wetness from his coat. 'Evenin'. I didn't expect anybody to be checking in this late.'

A pleasant mask fell over Grant's features.

'It's all right, Marshal. I was just leaving.' He touched the brim of his derby hat to both men. 'I'll see you around, Nicholls. Better make sure you're not clutching at air next time.'

Luke waited until the door closed, then allowed his legs to fold him into the chair. Remembering the doctor's advice, he measured his breathing, inhaling and exhaling slowly as he wiped his damp palms against his sleeves.

'I take it that was the infamous William Grant?' Dan observed.

With his heart rate returning to normal, Luke nodded and handed the marshal a cup of coffee, relieved to see that his hand wasn't shaking.

'He's not what I expected,' Dan commented. 'What did he want?'

'I don't know. Why does a cat play with a mouse?'

'You think this is a game to him?'

Luke shrugged, feeling sweat trickle down his back. 'I know it isn't to me.'

5

The clouds had lifted by the time Luke rolled out of bed mid-afternoon and headed over to the saloon. He stopped to peer over the split doors before going inside. As usual the place was half empty. There was no sign of Grant but tinkling laughter drew his attention to a table at the back of the room.

As if she sensed him watching her, Kate looked up and smiled before dealing two cards to each man at the table. Even in the dim setting of the saloon her face glowed and the green dress she was wearing made her eyes sparkle like emeralds.

Luke nodded an acknowledgement and pushed his way inside. When he reached the bar, Jim handed him a glass of beer.

'Your friend's a real draw,' the barkeep commented.

40

Luke thought about denying the association but decided it wasn't worth it.

'I can see that. Why's she here?'

'She asked if she could deal a few hands of blackjack if she gave the house a percentage. You know me, I never like to miss an opportunity to make money. Business has already picked up.'

'Has it?' Luke asked, casting a dubious look around.

'Hey, six customers is better than five.'

Jim walked away laughing and Luke turned his attention back to the table where Kate was putting the cards away in her reticule. Judging by the good-natured grumbling around the table, she had made a few new friends already.

'Howdy, sunshine,' she said, sidling up beside Luke. 'Buy a girl a drink?'

Luke noticed Jim smirking as he returned and poured a shot of whiskey. When the barkeep lingered Luke scowled until he moved off, still grinning.

41

'I didn't expect to see you in here,' Luke commented.

'A girl's got to make a living.'

For some reason seeing her dealing cards to a table of lecherous bums irked him, but Luke decided to reserve judgement. After all, what was it to do with him how she made her money?

'It bothers you, doesn't it?' she said. 'Me being here, I mean.'

'Why should it?'

'No reason, I guess. Maybe just wishful thinking.' She searched his eyes for a few seconds, then said, 'Do you play?'

The idea didn't appeal. 'I wouldn't want to take your money.'

'What makes you think I wouldn't take yours?'

A slight quirk of her eyebrow challenged him to find out but he decided not to accept. He was beginning to realize she had a comeback for everything and he didn't want to end up resenting her for it. Just then, a breeze wafted in as the batwings swung open. Luke glanced across, avoiding eye contact with the newcomer but noticing enough to decide whether he warranted more attention. He breathed deeply as Grant strode in, passing close behind him.

'Whiskey,' Grant said as the barkeep approached. 'And one for the lady. Leave the bottle.'

'I already have one,' Kate mumbled. Grant took it and drank it down.

'Now you don't.'

Kate eased in closer to Luke, who remained leaning on his elbows as her back brushed his arm.

'We came in on the stage together,' Grant reminded her as he watched the whiskey being poured. 'I told you my name, as I recall, but you never told me yours.'

'K-Kate,' she said simply.

Even without the slight hesitation Luke would have known she was uneasy. He could feel her trembling. Her reflection in the mirror on the wall showed that her face had lost some of its colour and she wasn't smiling.

'Are you a friend of Mr Nicholls?' Grant asked pleasantly; he slid the fresh drink closer to her.

She eyed Luke's reflection thoughtfully.

'I think so, but it's early days,' she said, her smile returning. She turned back to Grant. 'You?'

'Maybe . . . ' He tossed back his drink. 'When Hell freezes over.'

Luke concentrated on his breathing, forcing himself to take slow, steady breaths as he contemplated his own reflection in the mirror. Despite a rise in his heart rate and the feeling that his body was suddenly beaded in sweat, his outward appearance was calm, disinterested, unconcerned.

But he knew Grant was watching him, looking for a reaction as he reached across and brushed back a lock of hair that had fallen across Kate's forehead. His fingers lingered before tracing the outline of her cheek and mouth, his thumb stroking her lower lip. She pulled her head away but that didn't deter him. His fingers only moved to caress her neck, creeping lower towards the curve of her breasts.

'I'm not that kind of girl,' she said, slapping his hand away.

'No?' He grinned. 'I bet you could be.'

A tingle ran up Luke's spine. It was a familiar sensation. A mixture of excitement and trepidation. The prelude to a decision. It had been a long time since he had last felt it and he liked it now. But was he good enough to act on it?

'Hey, Miss Kate, are you coming back soon?' someone shouted from across the room.

'I'll be there in a minute.'

'That's the spirit,' Grant said, nudging her untouched whiskey towards her. 'Drink up.'

She recoiled from it. 'I've had enough.'

'I said, have a drink.'

'I don't want it.'

He grasped her hand, pressing her fingers on to the glass. 'I want you to drink it.'

'She said she doesn't want it,' Luke growled, without shifting his position. 'Leave her alone.'

Grant chuckled. 'It's too soon, but . . . I'm tempted. I want to know if you've got what it takes so bad I can taste it.' He swallowed Kate's drink, then slammed the glass down on the bar. 'But, no. The time's got to be right.'

Luke glanced uneasily at him. He seemed to be talking more to himself than to Luke. Rumour had it he had dispatched fifteen men since their last fateful meeting. Maybe the killing had driven him crazy . . . or crazier.

'Listen, I don't want any trouble,' Kate said, picking up the empty glass and shoving it towards the barkeep. 'Here, look, I'll have a drink.'

At the blackjack table, a chair scraped across dry boards and a tow-haired youngster dressed in a faded shirt, jeans, chaps and heeled boots headed for the bar.

'Everything all right here, Miss Kate?' he asked, looking between Luke and Grant.

'Fine, Lenny, just go back to the table. I'll be there in a minute.'

When he didn't move away, Grant turned to face him.

'Are you deaf or stupid?'

The cowboy gulped, his eyes widening, apparently seeing Grant's twin Colts for the first time.

'Deaf, *dumb* and stupid,' Grant concluded.

Kate gasped and started to move between them, but Luke wrapped his arm around her waist and pulled her along the length of the bar away from the imminent danger.

'Walk away, Lenny, please,' she implored the young cowhand. 'Nobody will think any less of you.'

'I can't do that, Miss Kate, unless this gent apologizes.'

Grant chuckled. 'All right then. I

apologize for saying you were deaf and dumb.'

Luke studied Grant's face. The look was new. A complete lack of expression. No curve of the mouth. No narrowing of the eyes. Nothing to betray his intentions. He could just as easily have been about to order another drink as kill a man. In that instant, Luke realized that Grant was the definition of a stone-cold killer.

And now the cowboy realized it too.

As he snatched for the old six-shooter holstered high on his waist, blood showed on his shirt. A spray of crimson spattered the old timer sitting behind him as the bullet ripped its way through flesh. The youngster swayed for a second then crumpled to the floor, already dead.

Kate turned and buried her face against Luke's chest; he continued to stare at Grant. Now that the killing was over, the gunman's mouth was twisted into a sickening smile.

'Yup,' he said, sliding a shell into the

empty chamber of his Colt. 'Stupid, just like I thought.'

Luke felt Kate's hand brush against his waist. He clamped his fingers over hers as she tried to grab his gun. She looked up. The colour had drained from her face, and even the tears couldn't disguise the hatred and frustration in her eyes.

Grant holstered his weapon, his stare fixed on Luke, the euphoria of the kill blinding him to everything but his victory.

'Bet you didn't believe I could get any faster,' he said.

'We've both had time to practise.'

Grant's mouth twitched into the semblance of a grin.

'Only difference is, tin cans don't shoot back.'

There was no answer to that, and Luke wrapped his arm around Kate and walked away. As they passed through the split doors and into the street, Dan Keen met them on the plank walk. He was carrying his new

Winchester and he levered a round into the chamber as he asked, 'What happened? Did you . . . ?'

'He just killed a man,' he said, not wanting to say Grant's name. 'Do me a favour and take my word for it when I tell you it was a fair fight.'

Dan frowned but he seemed to read the meaning behind Luke's veiled warning as he dropped the rifle into the crook of his arm. 'I'll be careful, but I've got a job to do,' he said, going inside.

6

Kate stumbled, dropping her reticule and spilling the contents in the dirt as Luke shoved her to one side of the split doors.

'What did you think you were doing?' he demanded, pressing her back against the wall. 'Did you think he wouldn't kill you because you're a woman?'

She chewed her lip, at a loss for words, knowing that trying to take his gun had been a stupid thing to do.

'Nothing to say?' He kept his hand on her shoulder as he looked past her, through a window into the saloon. 'That must be a first.'

The comment irked her, probably because it wasn't true. She wanted nothing more than to spill her guts to him, to spin a story so unjust that he would march back inside and kill Grant. But despite the weight of justification, she couldn't bring herself to threaten his life so recklessly after he had stopped her making a fatal mistake with her own.

'Nothing that would make sense to you,' she said at last.

'Do you mean I wouldn't understand why an attractive, intelligent woman like you seems drawn to trouble?' He stepped back and raised his hands. 'You're right, I wouldn't.'

'I have my reasons.'

'Don't we all!' He bent and retrieved her small velvet bag, taking the opportunity to peek beneath the split doors as he picked up the few items that had spilled out. 'Whatever they are, take my advice and forget them. Nothing's worth dying for.'

'I should take that advice from a man who makes his living dealing in death?'

'I'm just the night clerk in a run-down hotel. The only danger I face is getting a paper cut.'

Whether or not he intended to be

humorous, she relaxed despite his obvious apprehension as he continued to watch proceedings inside the saloon. She took back her belongings and repacked her reticule, pausing to sniff her handkerchief.

'What is that god-awful smell?' Luke asked, wrinkling his nose.

'Lavender oil.' She breathed it in one more time before shoving the wrinkled square into her bag. 'It helps with headaches.'

He shook his head, pointing to something under her foot. 'Is that yours?'

She bent and snatched it up without even glancing at the image on the bent tintype. It showed herself and Frank on their wedding day, standing stiff and straight-faced as they stared at the camera. After two months, the pain of losing her husband was still too fresh, bringing with it the memory of finding him gut-shot and left to die. It threatened to overwhelm her and she jammed the reminder back into her bag.

'I'm sorry I tried to take your gun. You're not the only one whose mind plays tricks when Grant is in the vicinity.'

'Don't be sorry. Be smart. Stay away from him.'

'I can't do that.'

She expected him to ask why but his attention was elsewhere. Instead he said, 'Then stay away from me because I've got enough trouble of my own.' He drew his Smith & Wesson. 'And my mind doesn't play tricks.'

'Are you sure about that?' she asked pointedly. 'You're sweating, your breathing's ragged. I bet if you held out your hand it'd be shaking.'

He glared at her. 'Ever think that might be a reaction to you?'

It was a cheap shot and she didn't react as she watched him push open the batwings ever so slightly, raise his gun and aim into the barroom.

★　★　★

Standing with his back to the bar, sipping whiskey and smoking a cheroot, Grant watched as two men lifted the cowboy's body and hefted it off to the undertaker's office. Immediately the barkeep swept up the blood-soaked sawdust and threw down a fresh covering to disguise the sticky remains, which were already soaking into the weathered floorboards.

After circling the room to ask for witness statements, the marshal returned to stand beside Grant. There was a glass of whiskey unattended on the bar and Grant pushed it towards him.

'I thought you might need that.'

The marshal shook his head.

'I've spoken to all the witnesses and, although I don't condone gun-fighting, it sounds like he drew first. The town won't be taking any further action.' He pushed the liquor back towards Grant. 'Thanks for the drink, but you can have it. I don't imbibe when I'm on duty.'

Grant left it untouched and straightened up. He was about two inches shorter than the marshal and he stepped back automatically to look him in the eye without having to bend his neck. He noticed the marshal's grip tighten on the Winchester as he eyed the twin Colts in Grant's holsters.

'They were a gift,' Grant said.

The lawman seemed unimpressed.

'You've already made up your mind about me, haven't you?' Grant said.

The marshal considered his answer then said in a measured tone, 'I judge by what I see and what I know to be fact. I look at you and I see a man wearing two guns. I know you ain't afraid to use them. Don't get me wrong though, I don't begrudge any man wearing a gun, Mr Grant, but this is a peaceful town. The last killing before today was three months ago and the one before that was almost a year. I'd ask you to bear that in mind the next time you feel the need to use those fancy Colts.'

Grant's mind whirled as he considered his next move. He wasn't worried about a threat made by a two-bit lawman. That Grant made him nervous was easy enough to see by the way he gripped his rifle. *Should he push him to see how far he was prepared to go?* Against his natural instincts, Grant decided to let the marshal have his moment, but not completely.

'Noted,' he said, 'but I won't stand around like a dummy if someone threatens me.'

The marshal frowned. 'All I can tell you is, if you kill anyone in my town make sure they draw first.'

'Did you give that advice to your friend Luke Nicholls?' Grant asked.

The marshal's steady gaze flickered ever so slightly.

Grant almost smiled. It had been a wild guess, based on their brief meeting at the hotel, but now Grant figured for sure that he had hit on something he shouldn't know. His fingertips tingled with anticipation as he waited to see how the lawman would react.

'I've had no reason to,' the marshal

said after a pause, 'but if it's necessary I will.'

Grant paid particular attention to the fact that Keen hadn't denied he and Nicholls were friends. That was interesting, something to be used at a later date maybe. For now, he turned back to the bar as though the conversation bored him, yet he couldn't resist one more jibe.

'Might as well save your breath then, Marshal. He couldn't outgun me on his best day and my worst.'

'Just remember what I said,' the lawman warned, walking away.

In no hurry, Grant considered this latest development as he finished his drink before following the marshal out. From under the shade of the plank walk outside the saloon, he watched the lawman mosey along Main Street and back to his office.

'I'll remember,' he said under his breath, 'but if you see me draw first, you won't live to do anything about it.'

7

Kate was gone by the time Luke had holstered his gun and ducked into a side alley. He waited for Dan to pass before he walked to the back of the buildings, taking a circuitous route to the opposite side of the street, where he ducked into the rear entrance of the jailhouse, locking the door behind him.

After glancing into the empty cell block, he bent his ear to the outer office, then went through. The shades were already half-drawn and Dan was securing his rifle in a gun rack on the wall. With a nod, Luke went to the pot-bellied stove and poured two cups of coffee. He handed one to Dan and took the seat in front of the neatly ordered desk.

Dan leaned back in his chair and took a deep breath; then, as if steadying himself, he let it out slowly before he spoke.

'I think I just met crazy,' he said.

Taking a silver flask from his pocket, Luke added a nip of brandy to each cup, then he waited for his friend to take a sip before he asked, 'What did he say?' he asked.

'Nothing you can't guess.' Dan shook, as if he were trying to rid himself of something physically abhorrent. 'He's made it clear he intends to kill you. There's no doubt in his mind he can do it.'

'Tell me something I don't know.'

'He's cottoned to the fact that you and me are friends.'

'Damn!' The coffee burned his mouth as Luke swallowed more than he intended. 'How the hell does he know that?'

'Perceptive, I guess. He must have put two and two together when he saw me at the hotel last night.'

'Or he was fishing.'

'Yeah, maybe. Don't worry about it. I

can handle him.'

But Luke did worry. Dan Keen was the best friend he had ever had — more like a brother really. Rightly or wrongly, Dan believed he owed Luke his life.

For the first time in years Luke thought about the first man he had ever killed: Ethan Keen.

Angry when he was sober, Dan's pa had been a mean son of a bitch when he was drunk. Ethan had been close to pistol-whipping Dan to death when Luke warned him to stop. In the middle of the Blue Bell saloon, surrounded by his cronies, the older Keen had slipped the six-gun back behind his belt.

'That's a mighty fine-looking gun you're wearing,' he'd said, eyeing the Schofield. 'Do you think you've got the nerve to draw it on a full-grown man, you little runt?'

Luke saw Dan stir, try to rise, but his pa's boot caught him a vicious kick behind his already bloodied ear and he slumped into a pool of his own blood. A tingle ran up Luke's spine but, as his hand moved to cover the gun shoved into the waist of his pants, he realized he wasn't scared. The racing beat of his heart, the tension that surged into every muscle and fibre of his body wasn't trepidation. It was anticipation akin to excitement.

'Oh, *hell* — '

Keen didn't finish whatever it was he intended to say. Neither did he manage to snatch the old Army revolver fully from its holster. Luke could remember clearly the way he had just stood there as blood spread across Ethan Keen's chest. When he finally crumpled at the knees and fell face first into the sawdust, a gaping wound in his back marked the passage of several .45 slugs through his body and into the blood-spattered wall a few feet behind him.

They had never spoken of it since, but Luke knew there was nothing Dan wouldn't do to repay him for saving his life.

'What about your lady friend?' Dan was asking now, drawing him back to the present. 'She looked pretty shaken up. Is she all right?'

Luke frowned. 'You mean besides being loco?'

Dan's expression registered confusion.

'She tried to grab my gun. I don't know what the hell she was thinking.'

'Did you bother to ask?'

Luke shook his head. 'She wanted me to but I was too damned angry and too busy watching your back to listen.'

'Appreciated.'

'Welcome.'

'So she didn't say why?'

'Just that she had her reasons for wanting Grant dead.' Reasons that were none of Luke's business but none the less played on his mind. 'It doesn't make any sense a woman like that trying to get herself killed.'

Dan gave it some consideration.

'Didn't you tell me she was a widow? Maybe Grant killed her husband. Revenge can be a powerful motive for stupidity.'

Luke understood that well enough.

'Maybe, but she said her old man was a gambler. It's more likely he played a bad hand.' Luke shrugged thoughts of Kate Portillo and her luckless husband away as Grant returned to the forefront of his thinking. 'Listen, I don't know what I was doing coming here. I've been chasing Grant or waiting for him to catch up with me since I got out of the pen, but I don't want to stir up trouble for you. Maybe I should leave town, take my troubles with me.'

'No.' It was a decisive response, but Dan looked at odds with himself. 'Y-yes. No,' he said, with less certainty.

Despite the tension hanging over them, Luke chuckled.

'You never were good at making up your mind.'

'You don't make it easy. On the one hand, it's good seeing you again. I like having someone to talk to who doesn't have a reason for being friendly with the marshal. But on the other, I don't want to bury you.' He sat forward in his chair, his expression serious, worried. 'Do you think you're ready?'

Honestly, Luke didn't know. The episode in the street and the doctor's diagnosis had shaken his confidence. He knew he was still good with a gun, but without the nerve to back it up he was no better than a greenhorn.

'You've seen me shoot,' he said, leaving Dan to make up his own mind. He pushed to his feet. 'I'm going back to the hotel. See you tonight?'

'Same time as usual.' Dan looked like he had more to say but after a few seconds he relaxed back in his chair and swung his feet up on the desk. 'Are you going to talk to your lady friend again?'

Luke stopped in his tracks. 'You mean Kate? Why would I do that?'

'Oh, I don't know. It just seemed to me like she'd got under your skin.' Dan reached for a stack of dodgers and concentrated on flicking through them, a slight smirk on his face. 'And now I've seen her, I can see why. Maybe you could talk some sense into her . . . or something.'

'I'm the last person who should be giving advice to anyone.'

'Are you sure about that? Seems to me she's been paying you a lot of attention. You might be the one person she will listen to.'

'I doubt it.'

'Try turning on the charm.' Dan grinned. 'You remember how to do that, don't you?'

Luke shot his friend a scowl.

'Seems to me like crazy might be contagious around here,' he said good-naturedly. Nevertheless, a thought occurred to him as he left as stealthily as he had arrived.

8

Locked in her hotel room, Kate sat on the edge of the bed staring at the oilskin-wrapped package beside her. When she had snatched it from the bottom of her old carpetbag she had thought she was ready to open it, but now, two hours later, her hands were still clasped in her lap and her anger had turned to quivering fear. She almost fell off the bed when a knock rattled the door in its frame.

'Who is it?' she called, grabbing the package and stuffing it back into its hiding-place beneath the bed.

'Luke Nicholls.'

She glanced in the mirror above the washstand, smoothed a few wisps of hair away from her face and wiped the wetness from around her eyes. A pinch to each cheek brought some colour to her pale complexion. A smile added some lightness to her voice when she called, 'Come on in.'

As he closed the door behind him, she saw his eyes take in every detail from the silk scarf draped over the head of the bed, the yellow wildflowers in a glass of water on the windowsill and the vials of rose water and lavender oil on the washstand. Finally his attention settled on her, his expression giving nothing away.

Lord, he reminded her of Frank. He was so much like him in his ways, and Frank had been difficult to read too. When it suited him, it had been impossible to know what he was thinking, and nothing about him gave any clue to his purpose. Just like Luke now.

She held his gaze, her well-practised smile belying her frustration as she tried to guess his motive for being there. Hadn't he made it clear he wanted nothing to do with her? Was he the kind of man who would change his mind?

'To what do I owe the pleasure?' she

asked at last, cordially.

He took a deep breath, blowing it out, but saying nothing as he continued to stare at her.

'Do you want me to guess?'

'I want you to leave town,' he said bluntly.

It was unexpected. For once she was stunned into silence.

'Listen, I know we don't really know each other that well, but I know Grant. If you're here to kill him, you'll fail.'

Strangely, she didn't feel angry. If anything, his interest in her motives gave her hope.

'And what concern is that of yours?'

'None, I guess, except you said you needed a friend and I'm being your friend now.' He reached into his coat pocket and crossed the room to join her by the window. 'Here,' he said, pushing something into her hand. 'It's a ticket on the next stage through, tomorrow at noon. You should be on it.'

She shook her head and tried to force the ticket back on him.

'You don't understand,' she said. 'It's taken me two months to get this close to Grant. I can't just walk away. He needs to pay for what he did.'

He crushed the ticket in her hand.

'Don't worry about Grant. He'll get what's coming to him. It might not be today but someday, somewhere, he'll challenge the wrong man.'

'You mean you?'

Luke shrugged.

'You're so like Frank,' she said. 'He tried to walk away from the gunman's life but it wouldn't let him.'

She fought the quiver in her voice, the sting of tears that threatened her resolve, but she couldn't control her need to reach out and physically connect with him. As she pressed her hand against his chest, his heart beat fast and strong beneath her palm.

'I don't want to see you die, but I don't think it will let go of you either,' she said. 'Heck, I don't even like guns and I can't walk away.'

'Don't try to understand me, Kate.

I'm not what you think I am.'

'What do I think?'

'That I'm some reluctant hero, but I'm not. I want to kill Grant as badly as you want him dead, but my reasons aren't as honourable as yours.'

'What do you mean?'

'I just need to know which one of us is the best.'

'I don't believe that.'

He backed away.

'Believe what you want. It doesn't change anything. Just know that whether it's me or someone else, he's living on borrowed time. We all are, those of us that live by the gun. But . . . ' he faltered, 'but you, you're a strong, good-looking woman with your whole life ahead of you. Don't waste it on a fool's errand.'

Maybe another time everything he said would have made sense but, with her flesh still crawling from Grant's touch, it felt like surrender. If Luke wasn't her ally, he was worth nothing to her.

'The only thing I'm wasting my time on is you. You're right, you're not the man I thought you'd be,' she said, turning away from him. 'I should have walked on by the first time I saw you. I won't make that mistake again.'

He opened the door and stepped out. 'I'm glad we finally agree on something. You've got a ticket for the stage tomorrow, so use it.'

She glared at his back as she followed him into the hallway and watched him walk away. He didn't look back and her disappointment seemed almost tangible as she went back inside and slammed the door.

'Damn you, Katie!' she said aloud. 'He was supposed to help you. Why did you let him walk away?'

★ ★ ★

'William Grant? Anyone seen Mr William Grant?'

Sitting alone at a table near the back of the saloon, the gunslinger looked up from his game of solitaire.

'I'm Grant.'

The lanky kid wearing a shopkeeper's apron and sleeve garters approached the table. He smiled and pushed back a flop of red hair that had fallen across his eyes.

'You got a reply to your telegram, Mr Grant.'

Grant eyed the envelope grasped between the kid's fingers. In his excitement the kid seemed to have forgotten that he needed to hand it over. Realizing his mistake, he thrust it forward.

'There you go, Mr Grant.'

Grant took it and reached into his vest pocket.

'No need, Mr Grant. Just don't forget, if you need any supplies of any kind, Brown's General Store. We're right next door to the telegraph office, just along Main Street on the right hand side. Big sign out front that says 'Brown's General Store'.'

With that the kid turned on his heel

and hurried out of the saloon.

Grant pulled a toothpick from his pocket and chewed on it as he studied the envelope. It was creased but otherwise intact.

Unhurriedly, he opened it and withdrew the single sheet of paper folded evenly inside. Slowly and silently, he read the content.

BE PATIENT STOP BRING HIM TO ME STOP NO MISTAKES THIS TIME STOP

He stared unseeing at the words, the toothpick splintering between his teeth as his jaw clenched. So the old man hadn't changed his mind. He wanted to see Nicholls die. But how the hell was he supposed to get him to Springfield? Not that he had a choice if he wanted to get back in the old man's good books. Not following orders had already cost him dearly. The old goat had refused to send him any more expense money until he located Nicholls, and

74

had even threatened to send someone else to do the job.

Temper rising, he screwed the missive into a ball, propelled it across the room, and swiped the cards and his unfinished drink off the table. Several faces turned towards him but no one challenged him as he stood and stared around the room. Seeing no immediate outlet for his anger, he kicked his chair aside and strode into the street.

9

From a bench outside the Beaumont Hotel Luke watched Grant storm out of the saloon and look both ways. A drunk sitting propped up against the wall beside the batwings said something to him, earning a kick that sent him sprawling into the street. As if nothing had happened. Grant again gazed along the street.

'What do you suppose has got him riled?'

Luke bristled as Kate stopped close beside him.

'Don't know and don't much care,' he lied, getting to his feet as Grant started coming along the street. 'But it looks like we're about to find out. You might want to get off the street.'

She blocked him as he tried to pass.

'Don't go out to meet him. I need to talk to you.'

'Talking ain't doing. I don't know why I thought it could be any different.'

'There are things you don't know that you need to know. About what Grant did to my husband,' she argued. 'And I need to know about you and him. Don't go.'

Luke rested a hand on his gun.

'It's too late for that now.'

She clung to his arm, trying to stop him.

'He said you were his friend. His name was Frank Portillo.'

The name didn't mean anything.

'I'm not interested.'

Shrugging free, he turned and walked on to the street, dodging between two wagons as they trundled past in opposite directions. It was a nifty move and she didn't follow.

'Frank Portillo,' she shouted. 'He said you were his friend. You need to know what happened to him.'

He kept moving, closing the distance between himself and Grant. Already he could see people starting to stare, to delay their plans as they backed up against buildings and sought to avoid the trouble that was brewing.

When he reached the middle of the street, Luke pulled his gun.

'I recall you asked if I'd turned yellow. You ready to find out?'

Grant kept on coming, closing the gap between them without a falter. Twenty feet. Fifteen. Ten. Closing in.

Luke changed direction, trying to keep some ground between them, but Grant mirrored him.

'Not here,' Grant said when he was within three feet. 'Not now.'

'What makes you think you're calling the shots?'

'I don't think, I know, and I'm telling you it's not happening here or now.'

Luke shoved him in the shoulder, stopping him as he made to pass.

'What's your game, Grant? You show up, you prod me and then what . . . you throw up your hands when I offer you what you want?'

'Your friend the marshal doesn't look too happy.'

Luke glanced across at Dan. 'He'll get over it.'

'Not if he's dead. You know how this works. We empty our guns at each other, but who knows where a stray bullet might end up.'

'Is that a threat?'

Grant shrugged. 'I'm wearing twin Colts. The odds are in my favour, wouldn't you say?' He straightened his derby hat. 'Walk away. Live to fight another day,' he said, continuing on past. 'I'll let you know where and when.'

Luke watched him. 'I ain't dancing to your tune, Grant.'

Grant carried on walking.

'Holster your weapon,' Dan said, stepping in beside Luke. 'What the hell was that all about?'

Luke spat in the dirt. 'I don't know, but he's up to something and I don't like not knowing what.'

'Maybe he's changed his mind. I was

clear on what would happen if he started a fight.'

'Grant doesn't care about the law.' Luke spotted Kate coming towards them and groaned. 'Not again. Cut her off for me, will you? She's becoming more trouble than Grant.'

He walked away, the hair on the back of his neck bristling as he headed into the hotel and to his room. He looked inside. It was a small, depressing space and he wondered why he put up with it. He slammed the door and went to the front desk.

'Hey, Orville,' he said, coming up behind the clerk who was reading a news-sheet. 'Is thirteen still empty?'

'Sure. The key's on the board. Help yourself.' The clerk didn't bother to look up. 'Are you expecting company?'

'No, just looking for a place to get some peace and quiet.' Luke took the key and headed for the stairs. He stopped on the bottom step. 'By the way, Orville, if Mrs Portillo in room eight asks where I am, say you haven't seen me.'

Orville looked up, his expression quizzical, but he nodded without asking why.

When he reached room thirteen, Luke locked the door behind him, took off his jacket and boots and reclined on the bed. With his hands clasped behind his head he considered the bullet-riddled and stained ceiling before closing his eyes. But if sleep had been on his mind it was elusive as his thoughts refused to exclude Kate.

It didn't take much to conjure an image of her smile and the playful twinkle in her blue-green eyes. They reminded him of sun-drenched pools of cool clear water. Yet his fanciful musings were tainted. What was it about the lavender oil she used that bothered him so much? Sure, perfume reminded him of the brothels he had visited as a youngster, but she had admitted she was no angel and who was he to judge? What was it then? Damn, she was an annoyance. Why couldn't she just take his advice, get out of town and leave him alone?

10

Kate felt a quiver of nerves as she entered the saloon. Would she still be welcome after what had happened? Her gaze moved to the floor where the new layer of sawdust showed traces of the blood that had been spilled earlier. She was about to turn and leave when Jim saw her and pointed to an empty table at the back.

'Looks like some of you gents are about to lose your hearts and your money,' he shouted across the room.

Heads turned and chairs scraped across dry boards as several patrons changed seats to occupy the table in the corner. Several others shouted encouragement.

'Nice to see you again, Miss Kate.'

'I hope you're going to let me win some of my money back.'

Feeling a little more at ease, she pulled her old pack of cards from her reticule and took her place. 'All right boys, what's it to be? Blackjack or stud? Although I'd have to warn you, I'm slightly better at faro than I am at blackjack.'

A couple of hours later, with the saloon filling up and men jostling to join her table, Kate excused herself and made for the end of the bar. Several men were lined up along its length, and when Jim was finished serving every one of them he ambled over to her.

'You're three drinks to the good,' he said, pouring whiskey in to a glass for her. 'All courtesy of the gent in the big hat, the bummer with the beady eyes, and Big Jack, owner of the Bent-T.'

She inclined her head in thanks to each one in turn, quickly averting her gaze before any of them could misinterpret her action as an invitation to join her.

'Here's your share, as agreed,' she said, handing over a roll of notes.

'Thank you.' Jim slid the money into a pocket behind his apron. 'You're very popular.'

'I wasn't sure I would be after what happened.'

'It wasn't your fault. That gunny came in here looking for trouble. To tell the truth, I thought it was going to be with Luke.' He shrugged. 'I guess men like that have their own code.'

'I guess so.'

Jim wandered away to serve another customer, leaving her to mull over his comments. When there came a lull, he sauntered back to tell her that she was five drinks in credit.

'I've had enough,' she said, pushing away her untouched glass. 'I think I'll call it a night.'

Jim nodded. 'You're staying at the Beaumont, aren't you?'

'For now.'

He reached under the bar and pulled

out a crumpled sheet of paper, folded into four.

'Would you give this to Luke?'

She looked at it, but didn't attempt to read it.

'Sure. I can leave it at the front desk.'

'I'd sooner you handed it to him.'

As she took it, a thought occurred to her. Maybe doing this favour might gain her a few minutes of Luke's time, an opportunity to explain and get him on her side.

'Tell him that Grant feller left it before he raged out of here earlier,' Jim added.

Suddenly, she had an urge to read it, but with men edging along the bar towards her, and the saloon's two whores looking daggers at her, she slipped it inside her reticule and made a swift exit.

She pulled her light shawl higher around her neck as she stepped outside and looked up and down the deserted street. Night had fallen, bringing with it a chill nip to the air. Here and there lamps had been lit but they offered little illumination. She stepped off the plank walk and made her way along the middle of the rutted road. Frank used to scold her for it, but she preferred to be out in the open, away from the shadows and the boogeymen that might lurk there.

A few minutes later, having reached the Beaumont without incident, she stopped outside the hotel to read the note in a meagre pool of light that penetrated the etched glass of the entrance doors.

BE PATIENT STOP BRING HIM TO ME STOP NO MIS-TAKES THIS TIME STOP

She pondered for a minute or two, although deep down she knew what it meant. Frank had been right. As he lay dying he had speculated that Grant was working for someone. Men like them didn't bushwhack each other, he had said; the thrill was in the contest.

Despite never having mentioned Luke Nicholls before, with his last breath he had told her to find him and give him the Schofield that he, Frank, had kept wrapped in an oilskin but had never worn. She hadn't known why — still didn't, but she did know that if she wanted to find the man behind Frank's death, Luke Nicholls was the key.

She folded the note and stepped into the hotel foyer. It was a few minutes before ten o'clock. Orville smiled broadly and smoothed his oily blond hair as she approached the desk.

'I'm looking for Luke,' she said. 'Is he in his room?'

'I haven't seen him all day. Is there something I can do for you?'

'No, I need to speak to Luke. Do you know where he is?'

The clerk leaned back in his chair, his gaze darting about. 'I haven't seen him all day.'

Orville was a bad liar and Kate had been lied to often enough to recognize one when she saw him. So Luke was avoiding her. After a few seconds spent staring at Orville, watching him squirm as if he would rather be anywhere than facing her, she reached across the desk.

'Do you mind?' she asked, picking up a pencil.

Quickly she scribbled a few words on the reverse side of the note. That done, she ignored Orville and went directly to Luke's room. She hesitated before knocking, noting that no light showed beneath the door. She pressed her ear against the thin wooden panels but no sound reached her. With a sigh, she bent and slipped the note underneath.

11

After eating a hearty meal in the dining room of the Grand Hotel, Grant changed out of his town suit and into jeans, a work shirt and a buckskin jacket. Wordlessly he paid his bill, and carrying his canvas travelling bag and clutching a felt hat at his side, he headed for the livery stable. No one was about so he let himself in.

He found the skinny old hostler, fully clothed, asleep on a narrow mattress in a room off to one side. The old man reeked of whiskey and when he didn't respond to Grant's loud wake-up call, Grant jabbed him in the ribs. He came awake with a spluttered curse, quietening down quickly when he recognized his visitor.

'Are the horses ready?' Grant asked.

'You betcha. And young Kit Brown brought over some supplies earlier, said you'd already paid and I was to look after them until you came by.'

Grant stepped aside so that the old man could get up.

'Where are the horses?'

Carrying a kerosene lantern, the oldster showed him to the corral where stood a chestnut mare and an appaloosa gelding. Both animals were saddled and kitted out with saddle-bags and a bedroll. A couple of burlap sacks and a bulky brown-paper package were on the ground nearby. Quickly, Grant secured his canvas bag to the back of the gelding and the sacks to the mare.

'We agreed one-forty,' he said, taking a roll of money from inside his coat and shoving it at the hostler. 'You don't need to count it.'

The oldster looked at the payment through rheumy eyes, then at Grant's Colts. He frowned and shoved the money inside his shirt.

'I guess not. Is there anything else you need?' he asked, moving to swing open the corral gate.

Grant took the reins of both animals and led them out, picking up the package on the way. Without mounting, he carried on walking. He didn't look back as he merged quickly into the darkness.

'Pleasure doin' business,' the hostler mumbled without sincerity as he shut the gate and limped back to his bed.

Ten minutes later Grant reached the edge of town where a weathered sign swung in the breeze. He tied the horses nearby, shoved the package under his arm and walked to the Beaumont. Standing in the shadows, adjacent to the main entrance, he turned the face of his watch to catch the light coming from the foyer. It was almost eleven o'clock. As the hour hand ticked confirmation, the door opened and the clerk stepped into the street, letting the door bang shut behind him.

Grant waited a moment to make sure the man was alone, then stepped out of the shadows and grabbed him.

'Do you know who I am?' he asked, slamming the startled man's face against the wall, knocking off his glasses.

The clerk made several guttural noises but no sound that formed words.

'Then you know I won't hesitate to kill you.'

'W-what do you w-want?' Orville stammered.

'A woman came in on the stage yesterday. Pretty. Green eyes. Do you know the one I mean?'

The clerk nodded as best he could.

'What room is she in?'

The silence was broken by the click of a hammer being ratcheted back as Grant pushed the muzzle of a gun into the hollow of the clerk's back.

'Room eight. First floor. Third door on the right,' the clerk blurted out.

'Good.' Grant pulled the gun away and released the hammer. 'What's your name?'

'Or-Orville.'

Grant clubbed him behind the ear

and blood was already mixing with the oil in his hair as he crumpled to the plank walk. Grabbing him by the collar, Grant hauled him into a side alley and dumped him in the deep shadows. Then he mounted the fire escape that led to the first floor of the hotel.

A couple of low-lit lamps mounted along the hallway afforded enough light for him to force the window and climb inside without incident. Quickly, he found room eight and tapped lightly on the door.

'Who is it?' a sleepy voice asked.

'Front desk clerk. Orville.'

'What do you want?'

'There's no need for alarm but someone smelled smoke. We're evacuating the hotel until we can check it out.'

There was silence for a few moments followed by the sound of movement. Light shone beneath the door as a lamp was lit inside, then a key turned in the lock. As the door opened Grant pushed inside, dropping the package as he grabbed Kate and clamped his hand over her mouth. Lightly he kicked the door to and dragged her across the room, his arm wrapped around her waist, pinning her back against him and limiting her struggles.

'If you don't want to die,' he said, pressing his mouth against her ear, 'keep still and do exactly as I say. Otherwise I'll snap your neck right now. Do you understand?'

She froze.

'I'm going to move my hand away from your mouth. If you make a sound or try to run, you'll be dead long before anyone gets here. Do you understand?'

She managed to nod and tentatively his fingers peeled away. He could feel her trembling, and when he was sure she intended to cooperate he released his hold completely. She sagged as her legs started to give way, her hand reached out for the support of the washstand, knocking off a couple of vials, but she made no attempt to run.

'Turn around.'

Slowly she complied. In the lamplight

her skin was pale, her eyes wide with fear. Her head wobbled from side to side in silent denial as her breath escaped in short gasps.

'We're going on a little trip.'

'I'm not going anywhere with you.'

'You'll do as you're told.' He slapped her, then pointed to the package on the floor. 'Open it and get dressed. You've got two minutes. After that I'll drag you out of here naked if I have to.'

Confident his orders would be followed, he locked the door then went round the room, turning over the water jug, opening drawers and pulling out her undergarments. He yanked the armoire open and pulled out her clothes and travel case, tipping out the contents and kicking them around without bothering to investigate them. Finally he retrieved a pair of short, laced boots from beneath the bed and tossed them to her.

By the time his work was done, she was dressed in a loose-fitting man's work shirt, canvas trousers and a shapeless coat. After waiting for her to pull on the boots, he took a small folding knife from an inside pocket of his coat and grabbed her hand. He slashed the blade across her palm.

She started to cry out, but a punch to the jaw silenced her as she immediately lost consciousness and collapsed. Grant grabbed her by the wrist and dragged her to the bed, allowing drops of blood to fall where they might before he smeared more on to the sheets. Satisfied with the scene of bloody violence that he had set, he gagged her and tied her hands, then hoisted her over his shoulder.

As a final touch, he pulled a scrap of paper from his pocket and let it flutter to the floor before leaving unnoticed the way he had entered.

12

After a long night shift, made longer by
Orville's not showing up, Luke had
crawled into bed only a short while
since. He was dreaming about blue-
green eyes and a playful smile when he
was awakened by the sound of banging.
Dressed only in his long johns, he
kicked his way out of bed and,
bleary-eyed, opened the door.

'What the heck's so urgent you've got
to wake me up at this time?'

'Get dressed,' Dan Keen said. 'You're
going to want to see this.'

Five minutes later, still fastening his
shirt, Luke followed Dan into room
eight. The carnage inside instantly
brought him to full wakefulness. He
noticed broken glass around the washstand, clothes strewn across the floor,
water from the washbowl seeping into
the threadbare rug. Then, as his gaze

circled the room, he saw the blood. The knot in his stomach tightened.

'Is she . . . ?'

'I don't think so. Here.' Dan handed Luke a scrap of paper. It was yellow and faded. 'I found this. What do you make of it?'

INNOCENT BYSTANDER DEAD AS GUNMEN FAIL TO SETTLE SCORE

Luke recognized it. The news-sheet headline had been waved in his face a dozen times during his trial. Even now, after more than four years, the words ran amok through his nightmares. What it meant in the present circumstances he didn't know. Kate had pretty much admitted she had come looking for him. Maybe it had fallen out of her things when the room was ransacked, but along with the blood it seemed like a deliberate taunt by someone else.

'Where's Grant?' For some reason there was no doubt in Luke's mind that the cocky gunman had something to do with the scene.

The question didn't surprise Dan. 'I sent Deputy Keegan over to the Grand to check on him. He hasn't come back yet.'

Luke moved around the room looking for something that might offer an explanation. He bent down to pick up the valise that Kate had been carrying when she arrived. It was empty, so he put it aside and turned his attention to the blood on the bed. As he knelt down for a better look, something hard dug into his knee.

'What is it?' Dan asked, moving in as Luke reached under the bed.

'Don't know. Let's take a look.'

Carefully, Luke unwrapped the oilskin, a grunt of surprise escaping from him as he sat back and stared at the contents.

'Marshal?' A swarthy man in his early twenties poked his head inside the room.

'Keegan. Did you find Grant?'

'He checked out of the Grand last night. I asked a few questions around town and found out he bought a couple of saddled horses from Bart Smith at the livery and some supplies from Brown's store.'

'Anything else?'

The deputy's gaze wandered towards the bed and the oilskin. 'Not so far.'

'Well, keep asking around. Find out if anyone saw him after he left the livery stable.'

'Will do, Marshal.'

Dan waved him away and pushed the door shut. 'This is all too much coincidence for my liking. Do you think . . . what's she doing with that?' he asked, peering at the customized Schofield .45 that Luke slipped from its holster and laid on the bed. 'How did she get hold of your gun?'

'She didn't.'

Luke drew his own gun and laid it on the bed next to the oilskin. The weapons were twins.

'Well, I'll be a . . . ' Dan muttered.

Luke continued to stare at them, his mind forming a conclusion that made no sense.

'Did you find her reticule?' he asked, looking around the room.

After a quick search Dan found it behind the bedside table. Luke tipped out the contents, riffling through the assorted items before picking out the tintype. He took it to the window and held it up to the light, scrutinizing the image. It was bent and scratched, the man's face barely recognizable, but the more he looked the more sure he became.

Dan handed him a handkerchief, one of Kate's. The familiar scent of lavender assailed his nostrils as he wiped the image clean. Even in the formalized setting of a photographer's studio, Kate's pretty smile triumphed. Suddenly Luke realized his heart was hammering, his fingers tingling, his palms itching with a sweat that was starting to break out all over his body. He gripped the windowsill for support.

'What the hell?' Dan sat him down on the bed. 'Are you all right?'

For a few minutes Luke fought to steady his breathing, eyes closed as he fought to regain his composure.

'Is this what happened before?' Dan asked.

'Yeah.'

'What did the doc say caused it?'

'That it was triggered by something. I thought it was Grant but it's happened since then and he wasn't around. I even told Kate it might be her.'

Dan pursed his lips thoughtfully as he looked around the room. After a few seconds he went across to the window and retrieved something. Without warning, he wafted it in front of Luke's face.

'Could it be a smell?'

Luke's heart started to race as the camphor-like reek of lavender hit him; testily he pushed it away.

'But why would that bother me?'

'Maybe it reminds you of something you'd sooner forget.'

Feeling steadier, Luke decided to

ignore it, at least for now.

'That's why her husband knew me,' he said, looking again at the tintype. 'His real name wasn't Frank Portillo.'

'So who was he, then?'

Luke handed the likeness to his friend and picked up the gun from the oilskin. It felt familiar, comfortable. Looking between it and his own weapon there was nothing to tell them apart. As far as Luke knew, only two had ever been made to that specification. Along with the tintype it left him in no doubt.

'Are you going to tell me what's going on?' Dan asked.

'Kate Portillo is the widow of one of the best gunmen I ever knew.' Carefully, he holstered the weapon and rewrapped it in the oilskin. 'You and I knew him as Ben Darby.'

'You mean . . . ?'

'Yeah. The man who taught me everything I know about how to use a gun.'

13

'Marshal Keen.' The door burst open and Deputy Keegan rushed in, red-faced and breathless. 'Come quick. Somebody's just found Orville Baker in the alley. He says Grant tried to kill him last night, left him for dead.'

Luke holstered his gun, grabbed the oilskin and followed Dan down to the lobby. A small group had gathered and Dan had the deputy clear them out, leaving only Laura-Beth, the hotel cook, who was holding a wadded towel to the back of Orville's head.

'How are you doing, Orville?' Dan asked.

The day clerk looked up, his eyes watery and a little unfocused.

'Glad to be alive.'

'What happened?'

'That feller Grant jumped me as I was leaving last night. Hit me over the back of the head and left me for dead.'

It was a flimsy explanation that offered no reason for an attack and therefore didn't make sense. Luke stared hard at Orville, wondering what he was hiding and why? Was he in some way complicit in Kate's abduction? Or was he holding something back for some other reason? Certainly Grant wasn't the kind to batter a man to death for no reason, at least not without an audience.

'Any idea why?' Dan asked, beating Luke to the question.

Orville's shoulders slumped and a look of anguish twisted his pale features. He swallowed hard several times, clearly finding difficulty in speaking as his lips moved without any accompanying sound.

'Take your time, Orville,' Dan told him.

Luke disagreed. Time was being lost if they were going to find Kate alive. He stepped forward, towering over Orville so that the clerk cowered.

'Did it have something to do with Mrs Portillo?' Luke asked.

Orville nodded, wincing as the movement added to his discomfort. Behind the broken lenses of his glasses his eyes rolled as he struggled with some inner turmoil.

'He wanted to know what room she was in,' he blurted at last. 'I didn't want to tell him but he pulled a gun on me.' Then he looked at each man, then at Laura-Beth. 'I'm just a hotel clerk. He was going to kill me. You understand, don't you?'

Laura-Beth nodded sympathetically.

Luke wasn't so understanding. He grabbed Orville by the collar.

'You gave her to that son of a bitch?'

Dan put a restraining hand on Luke's arm and took up the questioning.

'Did he say anything else? Say why he wanted her? What he was going to do?'

'No.' The clerk slumped back against the threadbare cushions and closed his eyes. 'That's all, Marshal, I swear. I've got a headache and I probably need some stitches. Can I go see Doc Bartlett now?'

Dan sighed and waved his hand towards the door.

'If you remember anything else, you let me or my deputy know right away, all right?'

Laura-Beth helped him stand, taking his weight on her arm as he stumbled across the lobby. Just before they reached the door, Orville turned.

'She was looking for you,' he said, directly to Luke. 'Maybe it had something to do with that note she had for you.'

'What note?'

'I don't know. She wouldn't leave it with me. I think she pushed it under your door.'

Luke left Dan giving instructions to his deputy and headed for his room. After a brief search, he found the note half-hidden underneath his bed. An imprint of his own boot suggested he had kicked it there when he came in. He moved back out into the light of the hallway and read the handwritten note on the outside of the folded paper.

This is bigger than you and me. We need to talk. K

He pondered the message before unfolding the sheet and reading the contents.

BE PATIENT STOP BRING HIM TO ME. STOP NO MIS-TAKES THIS TIME STOP

'What's it say?' Dan asked.

Luke handed the paper over and waited while the marshal read it.

'This just gets stranger. Any idea what it means?' Dan asked.

'It could mean anything but it doesn't change the fact that Kate's been kidnapped and somehow it's got something to do with me.' He stepped into his room and pulled out his riding clothes. 'Grant's got a good head start but I'm not a bad tracker.'

'That's what I thought you'd say.'
Dan nodded. 'I told Keegan to bring
your horse round with mine.'

14

Draped over the saddle like a side of beef, her hands tied behind her back and her feet bound at the ankles, Kate tasted bile but she knew that if she vomited she would choke to death before Grant removed the gag. They had been riding all night and, as if the dust kicked up into her face by the mare's hoofs wasn't bad enough, now the sun was rising, beating down relentlessly and intensifying the headache that had persisted since she regained consciousness just before dawn.

At some point she must have passed out again because suddenly the horse was standing still and Grant was pulling at her. She fell hard on to the dry-packed earth and lay where she landed, her cheek pressed into the dirt and her head spinning, her limbs too numb to move.

Grant left her there as he hobbled the horses, then made a small fire and set a shiny new pot in the flames. He didn't speak or look at her. No emotion showed in his expression as he stared off into the distance and waited for the coffee to boil. She noticed that he had only taken one cup from his saddle-bags. It was as if she didn't exist.

She moved her gaze away from him. Face down in the dirt there wasn't much to see, just earth and grass, but it was better than looking at him. Whether by accident or design, she was at least in shade. She closed her eyes, aware only of the pounding in her right temple, the taste of bile in her mouth and the lack of feeling in her extremities.

A tear slid down the side of her nose as she wondered how much she could endure. Her breath caught in her throat. She coughed, unable to stop, the dryness in her mouth making it impossible to swallow, until she gasped for breath that wouldn't come.

Cursing, Grant grabbed her by the collar and pulled her up, his fingernails digging into her skin as he yanked the gag away from her mouth. Then hot liquid burned her lips and tongue, searing her throat and adding fresh agony.

'Enough,' she gasped.

He let her go, standing over her, drinking the remainder of the coffee while she caught her breath. When she was breathing normally again, he looked down at her, his expression impassive.

'Do you think he'll come for you?' he asked.

She didn't answer. It was difficult to think with her head pounding like a drum. For a moment she thought he meant Frank, but despite her pain-induced confusion, she knew Frank was dead. She shook her head, trying to clear the fog.

'When I asked you, you said Luke was your friend,' Grant offered by way of explanation. 'Will he come for you, do you think?'

Luke? She didn't know. They hadn't parted on good terms, but if she said *no* then of what use would she be to Grant?

'He'll come for me,' she said, trying to sound certain.

'Good.' He swallowed the last of the coffee and kicked dirt over the fire. 'Then we better keep moving because I wouldn't like him to catch up with us too soon.'

He packed away the coffee pot and cup, then hauled her to her feet. She could see now that they had stopped in a stand of cottonwoods. Beyond was a meadow and somewhere nearby she could hear the gentle gurgle of a stream.

'No!' she said, fighting as well as she could, overcome with panic as he threw her over the saddle. 'Not again. Just let me ride.'

He held her balanced there with his hand on her backside.

'Can I trust you not to try to escape?'

She looked around at the open landscape.

'Where would I go that you couldn't put a bullet between my shoulder blades before I made it ten yards?'

'That's a good point, but maybe you've got nothing to lose.'

She strained to turn her head round and look him in the face.

'Maybe that's true, but there's something I want to see before I leave this earth.'

A shallow smile played across his thick lips, his dark eyes bored into hers as he pulled the small folding knife from his pocket. There was dried blood on the blade and he wiped it across the back of her thigh.

'Your eyes are very beautiful,' he said, 'but they'll never see me die, if that's what you're hoping for.'

She gasped as the blade slashed upwards. Her hands fell free, the sudden movement causing an agonizing pain in her shoulders.

'Keep still,' he ordered, slicing through the ties at her ankles.

With pins and needles replacing the

numbness, he shoved her into the saddle and handed her the reins.

'Whatever motivates you,' he said, 'just keep remembering: you can't outrun a bullet and I never miss.'

15

Luke and Dan found the remains of the camp five hours later. It hadn't been hard. Grant was making no effort to hide his tracks and one of the horses had a distinctive gait that caused its right forefoot to leave a drag mark.

'Seems to me that he wants us to find him,' Dan opined. He got down to inspect the ground. He touched the ashes lightly, then sieved them through his fingers. 'This is hours old.'

Luke surveyed the area without bothering to dismount.

'The light'll be gone soon,' he said, taking a swig of water from his canteen. 'We need to keep moving.'

Dan swung back into the saddle.

'Looking at the direction they rode off in, he's heading towards Holden. It's not much of a place. Just a way station, really. There's a trading post that doubles as a ticket office but not much else.'

Luke shrugged nonchalantly, although inside him the feeling of urgency weighed in the pit of his stomach like rotten meat.

'It's got to be worth a look.'

An hour later, with the day fading to twilight, they reached Holden. It wasn't hard to guess its history. Following the railroad line, they passed a small graveyard littered with simple markers. Scattered far and wide were the remains of derelict huts where once men with dreams had sought to capitalize on the railroad's expansion west. Someone had built a boarding house, but now all that remained was a false-front that proclaimed: *The cleanest beds this side of the Mississippi*. Now it was no more than a ghost town.

As the trading post came into sight, Luke immediately spotted two saddled horses standing outside. He pulled his gun and a quick signal from Dan saw the marshal ride off at a tangent, leaving Luke to dismount and lead his horse on foot. With each step his head swivelled, his eyes and ears alert for anything that might betray a would-be bushwhacker or give him some clue as to Kate's whereabouts. In the fading light nothing stirred but his mounting impatience.

An inspection of the waiting horses showed that the mare was the one with the uneven gait that they'd been following. Leaving his own mount at the hitch rail, Luke peered inside the squat building. Like the rest of Holden it wasn't much to look at, just a large single room with a few supplies lining one wall. On the other side of the room were a couple of tables and some chairs. Behind a long counter at the back of the room, a man of indeterminate age, sporting a bushy beard and hair past his shoulders, was warming his feet against a pot-bellied stove.

'Evening. Homer's my name,' he called out, kicking his feet into a pair of Indian moccasins and shuffling forward to lean his elbows on the counter. 'Come on in. What can I do for you?'

'Where's the owner of those horses?' Luke asked, standing his ground outside the doorway.

'Outhouse.'

'And the woman?'

Before Homer could answer Dan appeared around the corner of the building ushering another man ahead of him. Even without seeing the newcomer's face, Luke knew from his towering height that it wasn't Grant. As the pair stepped into the light streaming through the doorway, Luke saw that he was an older man, balding and flabby around the jowls. He nodded as he passed Luke and went inside.

'They aren't here,' Dan said. 'According to Finnegan, he bought the horses for a knock-down price and they left about four hours ago.'

'You boys want a cup of coffee?' Homer shouted out to them, already pouring from a blackened pot.

'Might as well,' Dan said, making his way inside. 'We aren't going anywhere until morning.'

Luke disagreed. 'I'll be ready to go out again as soon as I've had a drink and something to eat.'

Homer waved them towards a table. As Dan removed his coat, the man's close-set blue eyes glanced at the badge pinned to his vest, then studied each of the newcomers in turn.

'What did they do, rob a bank?'

'It's kidnapping.'

Homer's beard covered his chest as he pulled in his chin and wrinkled his brow.

'Who'd they kidnap?'

'He kidnapped the woman.'

'You sure about that?'

Luke sipped his coffee, allowing Dan to do his job while he kept an eye on Finnegan. The big man was standing near the stove, his gaze fixed on Luke, his expression quizzical.

'What do you mean?' Dan asked.

'Well, I'll admit the woman was quiet

and had a bruise on her chin, but she didn't look too upset. In fact, they sat right where you are and she polished off two plates of my rabbit stew. She even asked to use the outhouse and he let her go out on her own. Seems to me that if she was his prisoner he would have kept a closer eye on her and she would have made a run for it or something.'

Dan's expression was unreadable, but Luke knew what he was thinking. It didn't make sense, unless everything they'd seen so far indicated some elaborate ruse worked out between Kate and Grant to trap him. Somehow he couldn't bring himself to believe that. That day in the saloon, he had felt Kate's fear, seen the hatred in her eyes after Grant had killed the cowboy. Her emotions had been too raw and too real to be part of a nefarious scheme.

'Did they say where they were heading?' Dan was asking.

Homer grinned. 'Not directly, but he

bought two tickets for Springfield if that helps you.'

'Only if you tell me there's another train due that's going the same way,' Luke said.

'Seems like it might be your lucky day then, if you don't mind roughin' it.'

Dan exchanged a glance with Luke that said it wouldn't be the first time.

'There's a freight train due through in about forty-five minutes. If you don't mind riding in a stock car, you should be able to get a ride.' Homer ambled away. 'You'll have just enough time for some of my famous rabbit stew,' he called back.

While they were waiting, Finnegan shuffled over to them.

'Mind if I join you gents for a few minutes?'

Luke shoved out a chair with his foot and the big man lowered himself on to it.

'I used to be a gunsmith. Couldn't help noticing that gun you're wearing. Mind if I take a look?'

It was an unusual request, but Finnegan had asked nicely enough and Luke noticed that he only had the thumb and index finger on his right hand. His left was clawlike and twisted with arthritis. Even if he could hold the gun he wouldn't be able to use it. Without much hesitation, Luke handed it over.

Looking like an expert, Finnegan took a few minutes to assess it.

'Nice. Good balance. Fine craftsmanship, if I do say so myself. Only two like it.'

'Now how would you know that?' Luke asked.

Finnegan grinned. 'Because I'm the one that customized them.' He placed the gun on his palm and offered it back. 'I'm surprised to see this one without its mate. It concerns me some because I know the man who owned them. Man by the name of Ben Darby. It's a strange coincidence really.'

'Coincidence?'

'Well, that feller you're after, I

recognized those fancy Colts he was wearing, too. I customized them for Ben's brother Hank.'

Luke eased forward in his seat.

'Ben had a brother?'

'Had?'

'Ben's dead.' Luke filled him in with what he knew, although it was little enough. 'That man who sold you those horses killed him. The woman who was with him, she's Ben's widow.'

The big man slumped, visibly shaken.

'And you? What were you to Ben that he'd give you one of his prized weapons?'

'He was a friend of mine, my mentor you might say.'

'Makes sense. I guess that other feller would be Hank's pupil, then.'

'Why do you say that?'

'Well, I know Hank ain't dead, so it follows he gave the guns to that feller. Would his name be Bill Grant, by any chance?'

'He goes by William Grant, but I'm guessing they're one and the same.

What makes you think he's something to do with Hank Darby?'

'I know Hank. Whatever Ben did, he would do. If Ben trained you, then I'd bet Hank trained this other feller.' Finnegan scratched his chin. 'Interesting.'

'Why do you say that?'

'Well, it was their pa who had those guns done up for them. Son of a bitch was always pitting them against one another and when he died he left half his estate and a pair of guns to each of them with the message 'winner takes all'.'

'You mean he wanted them to shoot each other?'

'Yup. Like I said, a son of a bitch.'

'So what happened?'

'Ben wanted no part of it but Hank was like his pa. He wanted it all. Ben tried to walk away, told him to take everything, but that wasn't good enough for Hank. He needed to win it, prove he was the best. He forced Ben into an old-fashioned duel. They were both fast on the draw but on that day Ben's aim was straighter. One of his bullets took Hank in the arm, shattered his elbow and crippled him.'

'Ben never told me any of that.'

'He wouldn't. That was the worst day of his life. He'd crippled his brother and put a target on his own back.' Finnegan heaved himself on to his feet as Homer came back carrying a couple of steaming bowls. 'I'll leave you two to eat in peace, but I will say one more thing: it's probably no coincidence that Grant's heading for Springfield since that's where Hank is.'

16

It felt to Kate as if no time at all had passed since she'd rested her head against the window and closed her eyes, but the darkened sky told a different story. Her mouth felt dry and tasted worse than Homer's rabbit stew and she wondered how long she had been sleeping. A while, she guessed. Lamps had been lit along the length of the train carriage and she saw that she wasn't the only one to give in to the rhythmic chugging of the locomotive.

'Have you got anything to drink?' she asked Grant, who was sitting wide-awake beside her.

He reached inside his jacket, pulled out a plain silver flask and handed it to her. Deliberately, she wiped the neck on her sleeve before taking a swig. As the brandy hit the back of her throat, she came fully awake, her mouth coming alive at the taste of good alcohol. She started to take a second drink but decided against it when she noticed the woman sitting opposite give her a disapproving look and grip her Bible more tightly. She handed the flask back to Grant.

'How long was I asleep?'

He shrugged. 'Couple of hours. You snore like a pig.'

Warmth flooded her cheeks as the woman chuckled.

'I hope I didn't disturb you,' Kate said, addressing her.

'Not at all, dear. I've got a sister with the same affliction. I find it quite soothing. My name's Elizabeth. Are you travelling far?'

It turned out that Elizabeth was friendlier than she had looked, as she went on to tell Kate about her sister and how they had grown up dirt poor but happy. She was on her way to Springfield, where her sister ran a boarding house with her husband. Her sister had recently taken ill and she was going to stay with them to help out until she got back on her feet.

Kate felt Grant's irritation and, for the devilry of it, encouraged the woman to tell her more. Eventually, with a grunt of displeasure, Grant shifted sideways in his seat and closed his eyes. Not long after, the two women lapsed into silence, Elizabeth turning to her Bible for distraction. Once again Kate rested her forehead against the glass, set her gaze on the dark landscape, trying to make out shapes against the inky skyline. But there wasn't much to see and soon her eyelids closed under their own weight.

As though as part of a dream, she heard screeching. Flung from her seat, she collided hard with Elizabeth, struggled to gain her balance as the train braked. She glimpsed Grant, faring no better on his knees in the centre aisle. Around them, the other passengers were shouting, some in panic and some in pain, others scrambling to the windows to see what was happening.

Righting herself, Kate looked out. Somewhere up ahead a fire blazed, lighting up the surrounding area like a giant candle. The train had barely ground to a halt when several masked men burst inside. Moving through the carriage, they shoved people back into their seats as they spread out along its length.

'This is a robbery,' the leader shouted. 'You folks just do as you're told and nobody'll get hurt.'

Kate retook her seat and sat with back straight, eyes lowered. Beside her, Grant rested his hand on the Colt, which was out of sight of the bandit standing a few feet away.

'We want your valuables. Money, rings, necklaces, watches and anything else you've got on you. Just drop it all in the bags my associates are bringing round. If nobody does anything stupid,' the leader continued, 'we'll all be on our way in next to no time.'

Kate removed her wedding ring and placed it underneath her leg. When the bag arrived she held up her hands.

'I'm travelling light,' she said with an apologetic shrug.

Dark eyes narrowed above the bandanna that covered the outlaw's face, but after looking her over he switched his attention to Grant.

'I'll take them fancy guns you're wearing,' he said.

'You can try.'

The outlaw stretched out his hand but a slug hit him in the chest before he'd laid a finger on the gun.

'Hold your fire,' someone shouted. 'Hold your fire, goddamnit!'

The silence was immediate, broken only by intermittent sobs coming from somewhere further back in the carriage. Kate had thrown herself to the floor but, stealing a look, she saw that Grant was still standing, smoking gun in his hand. On the floor at his feet the outlaw lay dead, his glazed eyes staring in Kate's direction. She recoiled, glimpsing the dead man's gun beneath the seat an instant before she screwed her

132

eyes shut against the scene.

'Grant,' someone said. 'It looks like my payday just got bigger.'

'I'd like to say it's good to see you again,' Grant said, 'but it isn't.'

'Likewise. Drop your guns.'

'You know that ain't going to happen.'

There was a moment of silence.

'All right, empty the chambers, carefully, and then holster them or I'll blow a hole in your head. And don't forget to empty the spares out of your belt.'

Kate heard cartridges and casings thud and chink as they hit the floor.

Fresh footsteps sounded as someone new entered the carriage.

'We've emptied the safe, boss, let's — *Jesus!* What happened?'

Kate dared a look.

'He happened. Grab the bags and let's go.' The leader fixed Grant with a glare. 'You're coming with us.'

Grant's expression was steely but he seemed resigned to the situation.

'Do I have a choice?'

'Dead or alive.'

Grant swore and grabbed Kate's arm.

'Move,' he ordered, yanking her up.

She pulled back.

'If you know what's good for you, behave yourself. You might think I'm a son of a bitch but I'm molasses on a summer's day compared to these men.'

It was a poor argument. It was one thing to be Grant's prisoner, but being the prisoner of four men was a different kind of danger. Digging in her heels, Kate clung to the seat as though her life depended on it, which it might well do.

'Leave the woman,' the outlaw leader shouted. 'You won't have time for keeping company where you're going.'

Grant maintained his grip. 'If you want to collect on that payday, she's coming with me.'

The outlaw stared hard at Kate, a quizzical expression in his hazel eyes. All along the carriage, men were getting restless. It was one thing to steal gold and silver, but abducting a woman risked pushing a man to abandon common sense.

At last the outlaw nodded. 'Have it your way, but she'd better not slow us down.'

Grabbing Kate by the hair, Grant dragged her into the aisle. When she resisted, a hard backhand across her mouth rendered her senseless. She fell hard, hitting her head against the corner of a bench, pain splintering in her temple like breaking glass as the floor came up to meet her face.

Grant seized the back of her coat and she grabbed for the discarded gun beneath the seat. Although she had never had any liking for guns, Frank had insisted she should learn how to use one. It felt big and clumsy in her hand but she managed to hold on to it as she was dragged on to her feet. Elizabeth shrieked and lunged, distracting Grant who lashed out against her attack. With him thrown off balance, Kate yanked hard and he lost his grip.

She threw herself forward, hoping she didn't go straight through the glass as she hurtled into the side of the carriage. She hit it side on, stumbling as her shoulder jarred under the impact. Grant swore as he moved in on her, his eyes bulging in a face red with rage. Reacting on instinct to a hundred lessons, Kate gripped the gun and pulled back the hammer.

Never give 'em a chance, Frank had told her.

As Grant's fingers dug into her shoulder, she pulled the trigger.

17

Inside the filthy stock car, Luke listened to the horses shifting restlessly as rain battered like devils' wings against the roof. Although it was pitch black, Luke guessed that Dan was awake, going over what had happened and sifting through the information Finnegan had given them. His sharp mind was what made him a good lawman and friend.

'Did you come up with anything?' Luke asked as the darkness pressed in on him, bringing back memories of a small prison cell.

'Nothing. You?'

'Nope.'

Without all the facts, it didn't make sense whichever way you sliced it. Ben and Hank had parted on bad terms, but there was nothing unusual about brothers being estranged. Both men had passed on their skills and their weapons. The puzzle was why had Grant killed Ben and why had Hank ordered Grant to get Luke to Springfield?

'I guess we'll find out when we get there,' Dan said, shifting around in the darkness beside Luke. 'Might as well try to get some sleep. I've a feeling we're going to need our wits about us.'

Luke didn't doubt it, but sleep proved elusive. In the oppressive darkness his thoughts wandered inevitably to his time with Ben Darby . . .

★ ★ ★

The drifter with the fancy guns had ridden into Brown Town on a warm spring day. Slouched in the saddle and covered in trail dust, he looked weary and disappointed as his gaze scanned the sparsely populated main street. As he climbed down, Luke had offered to take care of his horse in exchange for a chance to handle the fancy Smith & Wesson that had caught his eye in the man's pommel holster bag.

'Sure, kid, why not?'

He passed it over, watching as Luke handled the weapon, switching from left to right hand with the ease of a professional juggler, all the while being careful not to put his finger against the trigger.

'You ever fire a gun like that?' the drifter asked. Luke shook his head.

'I never even held a gun before this.'

'You're kidding me, aren't you? You're a natural.'

'No, sir. After my pa was killed by a drunk cowboy shooting off his six-gun, my ma refused to have one in the house. She'd be mighty disappointed if she saw me now.' Reluctantly, he handed the weapon back. 'I just couldn't resist temptation when I saw that beauty on your saddle. It's mighty pretty.'

'That's one way of describing it, I suppose.' The stranger pushed back the front of his coat, revealing a second gun holstered at his waist. 'What about this one? They're quite a pair, aren't they?'

Luke was lost for words.

'Anything else you liked about it?' the man asked. 'How did it feel?'

'Feel?' Luke thought about it for a minute, about the weight, the fit of the ivory grip against his palm, the easy way the muzzle came up and the way his finger trembled in anticipation of squeezing the trigger. 'Like it was part of me.'

The man chuckled as he slipped the gun back into the holster.

'How would you like to learn how to use it?'

By the end of that summer Luke was wearing the Smith & Wesson about his waist and Ben Darby had moved on. By the end of that same year, Luke had killed Ethan Keen . . .

* * *

Drifting back to the present, Luke stood up to stretch his legs and ease the ache that was settling into his backside.

The weather had let up and now the chug of the engine ahead replaced the sound of the rain pattering on the roof. He leaned back against the board wall and closed his eyes, ready to pick up his thoughts where they had left off, but the squeal of brakes rooted him firmly in the present.

'We're slowing down,' Dan said, stumbling to his feet and sliding open the car door. He leaned out. 'There's something up ahead. Looks like another train.'

Not waiting for the locomotive to come to a stop, they both jumped out and ran ahead to join the small crowd of people milling about beside the track. In the dim light cast by the carriage lanterns, someone noticed Dan's badge, and within seconds folks had surrounded them, all talking at once and making little sense. Dan held up his hand for silence.

'One at a time. You,' he said, singling out a man with a sooty face and hands, wearing dungarees and an old Union kepi. 'You're the driver?'

The man nodded. 'Engineer.'

'Can you tell me what happened?'

In a thick German accent, the engineer told them how the train had been stopped, the passengers robbed and the safe carrying a large payroll had been robbed. Two of the bandits had been shot and killed. One passenger had been injured. In order to stop the train, the bandits had set a fire on the line and the rails had buckled, making it impossible for the train to go on. One of the passengers had taken a horse and ridden on to alert the sheriff in Springfield.

'The passenger who killed the outlaws, where is he?' Luke asked.

The engineer shook his head and shrugged. 'He vent vith the outlaws, that's all I know.'

An elderly woman with white hair, bright blue eyes and a cane hobbled forward.

'Seemed to me like he knew them. Had some unfinished business judging by the conversation.'

'How do you mean?' Luke asked.

'The leader called him Grant and said something about him being his big payday.'

Luke's heart lurched. 'You're sure he called him Grant?'

'I'm old, young man, not deaf.'

Luke nodded apologetically. 'What about the woman who was with him?'

'Dressed like a man, pretty as a picture? Turned out she had a lot more gumption than anyone else on the train. She put up quite a fight before they silenced her.'

'What happened?'

'I was too far back to see.' She pointed to a woman sitting by the track. 'But she was right there. They looked quite friendly. She could tell you.'

Luke left Dan to ask more questions about the robbery and approached the woman.

'Ma'am?'

Her head came up sharply, her pinched mouth and narrowed eyes giving her an angry look, but her cheeks were tearstained and her voice was small.

'Yes, sir?' she said, her gaze fastening on his holstered gun. 'Are you here to kill me?'

'No.' He sat down beside her. 'What's your name, ma'am?'

'Elizabeth Barnes.'

'My name's Luke, I'm with the marshal over there. I need to ask you some questions.'

She sniffled.

'Miss Barnes — Elizabeth,' he corrected, trying to put her at ease. 'I want to know about the woman you were speaking to. Did she tell you her name? Where they were heading? Can you tell me anything?'

A sob preceded another long sniffle.

'Kate was her name, but I talk a lot once I get started and she was interested. I didn't give her a chance really. You see I'm going to stay with my sister and — oh, there I go again!'

Luke didn't give her time to dwell.

'Did she say anything about the man she was with?'

Elizabeth shook her head. 'She didn't appear to like him much and the feeling seemed mutual. It struck me as a bit odd but I didn't like to pry. You meet all sorts travelling on the railroad.'

'I understand.' He got to his feet, his gut telling him there was nothing more to be learned. 'You rest easy. Help will be along soon, I'm sure.'

'Luke?' said a voice.

He had been about to walk away, but he turned on a dime. Stepping down from the train, Kate could have been an apparition. Dressed in ill-fitting men's clothes, her hair loose and tangled around her pale face, she looked small and tired in the meagre light thrown from the carriage windows. As she met him halfway, he winced at the deep cut across the bridge of her swollen nose, slowly noticing the dried blood on her lips and in her hair.

'Do I look that bad?' Her laughter sounded forced as she squeezed his arm. 'Grant got a bit upset with me. It could have been worse.'

'What happened?'

Dan came up behind them and gripped Luke by the shoulder.

'Seems like Mrs Portillo did something no man's been able to do. She put a slug in him.'

18

Grant had no idea where he was. They had been riding all night, the crescent moon offering little respite from the darkness as it passed in and out of low-hanging cloud. A light rain had started to fall before they entered the foothills, and by the time they emerged from the thick cover of oak into a large clearing, he was cold, wet and disoriented. With the moon slowly fading into a grey dawn and his moments of clarity becoming scarce, he was aware of a cabin and a small barn.

He almost fell from the saddle. It was the leader, Rickard, who caught him.

'Stay with me, Grant. I didn't save you from that woman so you could die on me now.'

Grant shook him off and staggered forward.

'Let's get one thing straight,' he said,

his fierce pride still intact despite the nagging ache in his side. 'This is your fault.'

Rickard's face stiffened. A tense minute passed as both men stared each other down. In the end, with his strength ebbing away, Grant conceded that his position was untenable.

'If you let me die, you don't get your money.'

'It might be worth it,' Rickard said, grabbing Grant under the arm.

Inside, the cabin provided no comfort. A partially collapsed chimney, two chairs and a small table were its only features. The dirt floor was puddled where rain had penetrated the sinking roof. Without a word, the men threw down their bedrolls on any dry patch they saw and broke out a coffee pot while Rickard tended Grant.

He ripped open Grant's bloody shirt and prodded the gaping wound.

'Another few inches and she'd have gut-shot you.'

Grant's jaw cracked as he bit down

against the white-hot pain that Rickard was taking pleasure in inflicting.

'As it is, the bullet barely touched you. It just ripped through the flesh, messy but not life threatening. You got lucky.'

He didn't feel lucky. He felt stupid. He had been shot by a woman and had lost his leverage with Luke Nicholls. Not to mention being saddled with Rickard.

'You gonna fix me up or talk me to death?'

'Don't tempt me. I'd as soon blow your head off as not, but it wasn't just me you stole from.'

Grant shrugged. 'Look on the bright side. There are only four of you to split it between now.'

'You're a son of a bitch, Grant, do you know that?'

'I'm the son of a bitch who has your money,' Grant stated.

Rickard stared at him. 'We'll get to that. First, tell me why that woman was so important to you.'

Grant could see the outlaw's mind working, wondering what might have been in it for him if he hadn't been so quick to drag Grant off the train without her.

'There's a man I aim to kill. She was going to bring him to me.' Grant said, feeling a fizz of excitement building in his stomach, making him forget the pain and his surroundings. His finger-tips tapped a staccato rhythm on the table. 'And after I kill him, I'll have everything I ever wanted. No question.'

'You mean he's another notch on your gun?'

'I've never notched my guns, Rickard, you know that.' His glance took in the pitted handle of the outlaw's old six-gun. 'It's a tinhorn thing to do.'

The insult hit home, and Rickard poured water from his canteen on to a neckerchief and smeared it roughly around the wound, inflicting as much discomfort as he could.

'Go on,' he said, a grim smirk on his face as Grant winced. 'It's your story.

Who is the man?'

It sounded like a dumb question to Grant, so obsessed was he, and he resented having to answer it.

'Luke Nicholls.'

'I never heard of him. You boys hear of him?'

Two of the other men, a Mexican and a weasel-faced youngster, shook their heads. The third, a tall wiry redhead in his forties, appeared not to be listening as he checked the coffee pot.

'If this *hombre*'s so bad,' Rickard said, pulling a shirt from his saddle-bags and tearing it into strips, 'why ain't we heard of him?'

Their ignorance, together with the pain that Rickard was inflicting, agitated Grant and his answer was no more than a low growl.

'He's been in the state pen for the past four years, but he's out now.'

'Seem to recall it was a run-in with you that put him in the pen in the first place,' the redhead chirped in, his gaze meeting Grant's curious stare. 'A woman died that day, didn't she? Stray bullet? Course, it could have been worse. You were lucky you didn't kill Nicholls . . . the way I hear it.'

It was an odd thing to say and it rattled Grant. 'You seem to know a lot about it, all of a sudden.'

The redhead shrugged and picked at his thumbnail. 'Holding up trains ain't my only line of work. I'm what you might call a free agent. One day I might be robbing a train, the next I might be working for a man who needs somebody found. You know how it is.'

Something about the redhead's overtly offhand tone bothered Grant. Everything he'd said — or hadn't said — was true. But how would he know that Grant hadn't been meant to kill Nicholls that day? It was a question that needed asking but the answer didn't need to be shared with Rickard, whose interest was already being piqued as he paused to listen more carefully.

Grant groaned more than he needed to, ensuring that Rickard's attention returned to the job in hand.

'Like I was saying,' Grant reiterated, 'he's been in the pen but he's out now and we've got some unfinished business.'

'All right, I understand that, but why drag the woman along?' Rickard asked. 'Why not just find him and kill him there and then?'

'Because,' Grant said, his fingers rapping a faster beat as Rickard wound strips of shirt around his wound, 'I need to get him to Springfield.'

'That makes no sense. What's in Springfield? Seems to me the place is barely more than a water stop these days.'

'There's a man there. A man who needs to see Nicholls die.'

'He won't take your word for it if you just kill him?' one of the others asked.

Grant slammed his palm down on the table. They weren't listening. They didn't know what was at stake and he wasn't about to try to explain it to them. Instead he went with a half-truth richly laced with contempt.

'You don't get it. You're just a bunch of . . . of two-bit thieves. This is about honour. Something none of you would understand.'

All eyes focused on him. He was aware of his breathing. It sounded loud and quick in the stunned silence. His chest heaved, his head pounding with a rush of anger. His fists curled into balls as he fought to control his temper.

'You're talking to me about honour?' Rickard asked, grinning with amusement. 'You, the man who stole a thousand dollars from me.' He laughed uproariously. 'For such a serious critter, you sure do make me laugh, Grant.'

Picking up the canteen, Rickard went to the doorway and washed Grant's blood off his hands.

'I still don't see why you needed the woman.'

'No, you *don't* get it, Rickard. I'm the best there's ever been. Nicholls won't show his face unless I make him. That's why I needed the woman. She was my insurance.'

Rickard slammed the door as a fresh downpour of rain slanted in.

'I'll tell you what, Grant. We'll ride into Springfield with you. If Nicholls ain't there after what you did to that woman, I'll forget about the money you owe me and help you find him.'

It was something to think about. Grant didn't want any help but, knowing Rickard and carrying two empty guns, he knew there was no point in arguing. There would be time to deal with him later. What he needed now was sleep, a few hours to regain his strength. Someone handed him a cup of coffee and Rickard added a splash of whiskey from a small bottle he pulled from his pocket.

'Do we have a deal?'

Grant nodded, regretting it for only a split second as the room slanted and the table came up to meet him.

19

A cold, wet night gave way to a dull, damp morning for the train's stranded passengers. Alongside the track, men built makeshift fires and people who had been strangers only a few hours before huddled together for warmth and watched the horizon. A spontaneous cheer erupted when a small team arrived around mid-morning to repair the track. Shortly before noon, the train rolled into Springfield. Elizabeth insisted that Kate must stay at her family's boarding house to recuperate from her injuries and the two women headed off, leaving Luke and Dan to find the sheriff.

Looking around, Luke could see that, once upon a time, someone might have had plans for Springfield.

Standing adjacent to the train tracks, its wide main street offered a general store, a barber, a newspaper office, a two-storey hotel, a saloon, the sheriff's office and a bank. Several other lots were marked out here and there; some even showed the first signs of construction but, as they passed by, Luke noticed that the wood looked old and weathered.

Standing opposite the saloon, the jail was a large squat building comprising one room with a desk, chair and stove, and an area at the back separated by floor-to-ceiling iron bars. When they entered, a lethargic deputy roused briefly from his nap to tell them the posse was long gone and assure them that the sheriff wouldn't need any extra help, 'especially from a marshal well outside his own jurisdiction'.

'If I was you, I'd rest up your horses then get something to eat and enjoy your free time,' he said, yawning as he reclined back in his chair. 'And close the door on your way out.'

With that, he placed his bootless feet up on the desk and pulled his hat down over his eyes. Convinced there was no point in wasting any more time on him, they left without another word.

'Maybe we'll have more luck at the livery stable,' Luke suggested as they headed back towards the outskirts of town.

He couldn't have been more wrong.

'I've got nothing I can rent you. The posse took every spare animal I had except for Mabel,' the old hostler said, patting the docile animal on a hind-quarter. 'And she won't do you no good, that's why they left her.'

Luke had to agree he could see why. The swayback mare with the gentle expression looked about ready to keel over. If he took her, she'd be lucky to make it to the town limits, but his sympathy for the horse didn't temper his vexation.

'There must be somewhere else where we can hire a couple of horses,' he said, the edge in his voice punctuating each word. The oldster spat a stream of tobacco juice. 'It ain't for me to say.'

'How do you figure?'

'Well, I wouldn't be much of a businessman if I sent customers to my rivals.'

'But we're not your customers. You don't have any horses to . . . '

Dan grabbed Luke's arm and turned him aside. 'Take it easy. This ain't getting us anywhere. I know you want to find Grant after what he did to Kate, and so do I, but standing here arguing ain't getting us anywhere.'

Luke scowled at the hostler, who smiled and shrugged.

'We're both tired and hungry,' Dan continued. 'How about we get something to eat and make some enquiries at the same time?'

It didn't sit well with Luke, but Dan had always been the brains in their friendship and he made sense now.

They left the hostler with instructions to take good care of their horses and, on his recommendation, headed for Big Sam's eatery. It was aptly named and the giant of a man who owned the place directed them to a table by the window. Being situated facing the main street, it afforded them a good view, and as they tucked into a late breakfast with copious amounts of coffee, Luke's anger started to subside.

'Did you see that?' Dan asked, nodding towards the saloon on the opposite side of the street. 'That old hostler went in five minutes ago and came out not two minutes later.'

'What of it?'

'Since he left there's been someone standing outside watching this place.'

Luke shoved his plate away and followed his friend's gaze. He didn't need to ask if he was sure. The big galoot in the undersized suit and oversized boots, his oiled hair glistening in the sunlight, wasn't making any attempt to hide his interest. Becoming aware that they were watching him, he straightened from his slouched position against the wall and, after pointing at them, curled his finger in a gesture that indicated they should go across.

'What do you think?' Dan asked.

'I'm guessing there's somebody in there that wants to see me. We know it's not Grant.'

'Darby?'

Luke slipped the Schofield from its holster and thumbed a cartridge into the empty chamber under the hammer.

'I think we should find out.'

Big Sam had been about to clear the table but he stepped back, his eyes drawn to the gun.

'You're the one he's been waiting for,' he said.

'Who? And how do you know I'm the one?'

Big Sam edged backwards, apparently wishing he hadn't opened his mouth as he stammered over the answer. 'H-hank Darby. He said you'd be wearing a gun like that.'

'What else did he say?'

'That anybody who saw you should let him know.'

Luke exchanged a *you were right about the hostler* glance with Dan.

'And? What else?'

Sam shook his head. 'That was it. Just to let him know you were in town.'

Luke digested the information. It wasn't surprising.

'Just one more thing,' he said as Sam tried to back away. 'Who's that feller over there who's been watching us?'

Sam didn't bother to look. 'That'll be Clyde. He works for Mr Darby.'

'Doing what?'

'Making sure Mr Darby gets what he wants, mostly.'

Luke looked across at Clyde. Standing straight, he was probably over six feet, thick-built and powerful-looking once you got past the get-up he was wearing. Luke couldn't see a gun on him but that didn't necessarily make him any less of a threat.

'How much do we owe you for the meal?'

'Nothing. It's on the house.' With that, Big Sam left the plates and disappeared behind the curtain that concealed the kitchen.

'Are you sure this is the way you want to handle it?' Dan asked, checking the chambers of his six-gun.

'If prison taught me one thing, it's that you can't avoid the inevitable. Better to face it head on than wait for it to catch you unawares.'

Dan nodded, unpinned the star from his vest and slipped it in his coat pocket. 'Then let's go and see what the man has to say.'

20

Clyde's pale eyes never left them as they crossed the street and mounted the plank walk. Close to, it was obvious that his nose had been broken a few times and, as he alternately cracked the knuckles of one hand against the palm of the other, Luke noticed calloused scars on them. When he turned to push open the batwings, a lumpy right ear confirmed Luke's suspicions that the man was a fighter.

He stepped aside so that they could pass.

'Go ahead,' he said with an Irish brogue. 'Mr Darby's waiting for you inside.'

'I think you should go in first.'

Clyde grunted. 'Whatever you say.'

Once inside, he pointed to a table at the back where two well-dressed gents were talking over a bottle of whiskey.

Besides them there were three men drinking at the bar, two others playing cards at a table near the door and a whore asleep at the piano. As Clyde peeled away towards the barkeep, Dan stayed back, watching the room as Luke headed for the table at the back. As he approached, the man facing him stood up and walked away grinning.

'Take a seat,' the other man said without turning round. 'No reason we can't be civilized.'

Despite the circumstances that had brought him there, Luke felt a tingle ripple down his spine as recognition replaced fear of the unknown. As he sat down, he forgot that this was the man who had sent a cold-blooded killer after him. Instead, he saw a man he knew. Sure, the years hadn't been kind to him. He was missing an arm, his face was thinner, the lines deeper, the hair greyer, but this was no dead man.

'Ben?'

'Come now, Mr Nicholls, you know Ben's dead.' Using his left hand, he poured whiskey into a fresh glass and slid it across the table. 'I'm his twin brother, Hank.'

In his gut, Luke knew it was the truth but it didn't make the similarity any less startling. He dropped into the recently vacated chair and downed the drink in one gulp, his eyes never leaving the familiar-looking face. In turn, Hank leaned forward and studied him, his gaze pausing when it reached the Schofield. He licked his lips, looking almost mesmerized by it, then snapping out of whatever reverie had gripped him, he relaxed back in his chair.

As his coat fell open, Luke noticed he wasn't wearing a gun.

'Disappointed?' Hank asked, coughing discreetly into a handkerchief. 'Did you think you would come in here and we would fight it out?'

'I didn't know what to expect — but if it came to that, yes.'

'I can assure you it won't. My fighting days ended when Ben put a bullet through my elbow and the sawbones did the rest.' He indicated where his right arm should have been, but where only a stump filled an otherwise empty sleeve. 'I never was much good with my left hand.'

'Then why go to the trouble of getting me here? I assume it was you pulling Grant's strings.'

Hank dabbed at his brow and upper lip.

'To settle an old score.'

'What old score? Until today I'd never met you. Until yesterday I'd never even heard of you.'

'Not between you and me. Between Ben and me. Unfortunately, Ben died before . . . ' A fit of coughing gripped him and he covered his mouth.

'You mean Grant killed him,' Luke corrected.

It was a moment before Darby was able to speak again, and when he shifted the handkerchief Luke noticed blood on it.

'That was unfortunate,' Darby said, slightly out of breath. 'I wanted Ben to be there at the end but he had a change of heart and William's loyalty to me clouded his judgement.' He shrugged. 'But what's done is done. The details remain the same.'

It made no sense to Luke. 'So where do I come into it?'

'That's obvious, isn't it?'

Luke shook his head and Hank smiled, as though he was about to deliver good news.

'Ben trained you and I trained William. It was what we agreed on. A final showdown. Winner takes all.'

'Takes all of what?'

'Not as much as there used to be, but enough to keep a man comfortable for a few years. The Darbys own half this town, for what it's worth, not to mention a small stake in the railroad. As sole remaining heir, that would all belong to you in the event of my death.'

'Heir?'

'You and William are both named, but only one of you can collect.'

'That's crazy!' Luke gasped in disbelief.

'Is it? Do you really think Ben taught you everything he knew and gave you a customized gun out of the kindness of his heart?'

Luke had never really thought about it. Why would he? Ben had never talked about his past or his plans for the future. He had just nurtured a boy's raw talent and never asked Luke for anything in return. In the end he had set him on the path, then left him to make his own way.

Luke shook his head, still unwilling to believe that Ben would have been part of such a twisted scheme.

'I can see this has come as a shock,' Hank said, 'but, like it or not, it's the way it's going to be. The stakes are high but so's the pay-off. My advice to you would be to make the most of the time you have left before William gets here.' With the aid of a silver-topped cane, Hank lumbered to his feet, the movement drawing Clyde away from the bar.

'And just so we're clear,' Hank went on, 'if you try to kill me or leave town or bushwhack William before the showdown, my men have instructions to stop you by any means short of killing you.'

Looking into his cold grey eyes, there was no doubt in Luke's mind that the threat was real.

'What if Grant doesn't show?'

'Do I look like a man who leaves anything to chance?' Hank started to turn away, then hesitated. 'By the way, do you have it?'

'Have what?'

'The other gun. Ben's gun.'

Maybe it was pure orneriness or maybe it was the hint of expectation in Darby's voice, but Luke decided to lie.

'Ben only gave me the one.'

'That's a pity. I'd like to have seen them together again after all these years. I guess some things aren't meant to be.' Hank sounded genuinely regretful as he shuffled away. 'Then again,

170

maybe that just means you're only half as good as he was.'

21

The aroma of coffee and a poke in the shoulder woke Grant with an unpleasant start. His eyelids fluttered against weak shafts of daylight that penetrated the shack's rambling structure. Flicking his tongue across dry lips, he tried to swallow away the bitter taste and texture that furred his mouth but it was a pointless effort. When he moved to a sitting position on the dirt floor, a stab of pain in his right side reminded him that everything that had happened had been real, and not some perverse nightmare.

'Sleep well?' Red asked, shoving a cup of coffee into his hand.

'Well enough. What time is it?'

'Around ten. Rickard let you sleep in. He didn't want you slowing us down.'

'Considerate of him.' The cabin was

deserted except for the two of them. 'Where is he?'

'Outside getting ready to leave.' Red chuckled. 'He has no idea what he's riding into.'

As the grogginess of sleep cleared, Grant remembered last night's conversation. He had said more than he should, but whether it would bite him in the butt remained to be seen. Using the roughly boarded wall for support, he pulled himself up and gingerly stretched the stiffness out of his body.

'Are you working for Hank?'

Red nodded. 'Only insofar as he told me to keep an eye out for you. Seems he thought you might have some trouble getting Nicholls to Springfield. Told me to help in any way I could if we crossed paths.'

Hank's lack of faith needled him but, given his current circumstances, Grant wasn't about to argue.

'Good,' he said. 'You can start by giving me some ammunition.'

Red chuckled. 'So you can kill me

when you kill them? I don't think so.'

'I thought you were here to help me?'

'And I will, when I know you ain't likely to put a bullet in me while you're putting bullets into them. In the meantime, relax. I've got you covered.' He backed up and walked outside. 'There's more coffee on the stove if you want it. We'll be leaving as soon as the horses are saddled.'

Two hours later they rode out of the foothills and on to open range that would eventually bring them to Springfield. Grant and Rickard rode at the head of the group. It seemed they had said everything that needed to be said and all that remained between them was a wall of stony silence. It suited Grant. If he had his way, and a loaded gun in his holster, it would be a permanent situation.

22

'Best rooms in the hotel,' the desk clerk had boasted, 'compliments of Mr Darby.'

But as Luke paced from papered wall to papered wall of the adequately appointed suite it felt like any other prison.

Glancing across at Dan, asleep on the high-framed brass bed, he envied him the peace of mind that allowed him the luxury. Even in the old days, before Ben Darby had arrived, Luke had been plagued with nightmares. What boy wouldn't be after seeing his pa's brains splattered across the plank walk? Yet Dan lived with a similar history and seemed at peace with it. The only difference was he hadn't actually seen Luke end his bullying father's miserable life. That was the only time Luke could be grateful to Ethan Keen for beating his son senseless. Maybe if that had been the end of it, time might have soothed Luke's mind too but the woman he had killed four years ago, Lucy Johnson — her death had been unnecessary and he couldn't forgive himself for that.

Dan stirred, his eyes unfocused as he took a minute to recognize his surroundings. He frowned when his gaze finally settled on Luke.

'You've got that look on your face,' he said.

'What look?'

'The one that says you're going through with it.' Dan got up and stretched the kinks out of his back. 'You're going to wait for Grant to show up because you know he will, half dead or not, and then you're going to kill him.'

It sounded judgmental, harsh, tinged with disappointment.

'That's why I'm here, isn't it?' Luke said, roughly. 'It's why Ben gave me this gun and taught me how to use it. It's what I do.'

'I know what you do. But knowing doesn't make it any easier.'

Luke was hardly listening as he drew the Smith & Wesson from its holster and stared at it lying on the palm of his hand. Even now it was still a thing of beauty to him. Over the years, hours of practice had worn the ivory handle to a brown lustre and there were signs of rubbing on the silver where it had been holstered. It had taken time and patience to restore it to full glory after it too had been imprisoned in a lockbox for four years.

'You've only got Hank Darby's word for it that Ben's motives were anything other than genuine,' Dan persisted.

'But you've got to admit there's a ring of truth to it. Why else would Ben have bothered with a kid like me? This is his legacy. The legacy of a gunfighter.'

'Bullcrap! There could have been a hundred reasons. You'll never know for sure, but why believe the first story you hear?'

Luke shrugged, losing patience with

his friend's balanced reasoning. 'Whether I do or not, it doesn't change anything. Grant and me have had our own score to settle for a long time. There's only one thing that's bothering me.'

'Kate?'

Luke holstered the gun and went to stand by the tall windows that opened out on to a narrow balcony. He was hoping that the evening breeze that wafted the curtains would cool his temper. It didn't, and he turned away and threw himself down in a chair. A bottle of whiskey and two glasses on a silver-plated tray stood on a small table next to him and he poured himself a drink, gulping it down in one, refilling the glass and repeating the exercise.

Dan came over to him and corked the bottle before Luke could take another refill.

'Have you got a plan that doesn't involve drinking yourself into a stupor?' he asked, sitting down.

'Kill Grant.'

'Yeah, I think you made that clear

already. I was thinking more about Kate. Darby doesn't know who she is yet, but he'll find out when Grant gets here. She won't be safe.'

It had been one of the things on Luke's mind since he had first surveyed the street when they arrived. At a glance he had identified two men watching the hotel. They were making no secret of it with their rifles held in full view, their vantage points giving them a clear view of the hotel's entrance and the window of his room directly above. When he had first pulled back the curtain, one of the men, a squat youngster with a head of curly black hair, had grinned and raised his hand in a pseudo-friendly acknowledgement.

'It's a sure bet they've got every way out of here covered,' Luke said, 'and everybody in town knows who I am and seems to be working for Hank Darby, so we can't expect any help.'

Dan frowned. 'Free food, free accommodation in the fanciest rooms in the best hotel in town, such as it is. Everything 'on the house' as the desk clerk put it. However you look at it, Darby's got us corralled.'

Luke nodded pensively.

'I know that look too.' Dan leaned forward in his seat. 'You've got an idea but I'm not going to like it so best just spit it out.'

Luke wasn't sure he liked it either, but there were lots of reasons why it was the best one under the circumstances.

'Darby said I couldn't leave town. He didn't say anything about you. You could take Kate and get out of here.'

Dan put his face in his hands while he considered it. Luke knew there would be a dozen objections forming in his mind.

'I know you want to cover my back but let's face it, Dan, until Grant gets here nothing's going to happen. Even then, what are you going to do? In the end it's always been me against him.'

Dan's sigh suggested resignation and

misgivings. 'Do you think when this is over Darby's gonna let you just walk away?'

'I honestly don't know. I just know I can't have another woman's death on my conscience.'

'I know it's a heavy burden you're carrying, but you can't let what happened to Lucy Johnson dictate the decisions you make now. Kate isn't Lucy.'

Most of the time, Luke tried not to think about Lucy in too much detail but in the back of his mind, something that Dan had just said niggled him. It didn't take much effort to bring her back into full focus.

* * *

A plump little woman with a head of errant brown curls and a smile as wide as the Mississippi, she hadn't let his reputation stop her from striking up a conversation. With her arms full of groceries, she had bumped into him as

181

they passed on the plank walk outside the store and a can of peaches had landed at his feet. When he handed it to her, her liquid brown eyes had met his without a flicker of hesitation.

'Thank you. I'm so clumsy, I've only got myself to blame,' she said. 'I go to the store for one thing and come out with ten every time.'

'No trouble at all, ma'am. Maybe I could give you a hand carrying them to wherever you're going.'

She had been surprised at that, blushing more at her own good fortune than the unsuitability of the man who had made the offer.

'I'm sorry. That's probably completely wrong with me being . . . new in town.'

'Not at all.' Her cheeks dimpled as she smiled. 'Being new in town doesn't make you any less of a gentleman, does it?'

They both knew that wasn't the problem. Already their meeting was causing people to stop and stare, to assume that he was bothering her.

'I hope not but, if I am a gentleman, I think allowing you to pass would be the more gentlemanly course of action if you want to keep your reputation intact.'

There had been some sadness in her eyes as she nodded. Shifting her groceries to the crook of one elbow, she had leaned in close and squeezed his arm before walking by.

★   ★   ★

Now Luke recalled where he had smelled lavender before. He remembered that the scent had lingered long after Lucy had left him there feeling better about himself than he had in a long while.

He picked up his coat and shrugged into it.

'I'll go for a walk. When they follow me, assuming they follow me, you can head out and talk to Kate. If you can get her away from here, do it.'

'What about you?'
'I'll think of something.'

*   *   *

184

23

When Luke pushed through the split doors of the Horseshoe saloon, every head in the smoke-filled room turned his way. Gamblers, cowboys, businessmen all stopped what they were doing to stare at the newcomer. As news of his arrival reached the piano player, he finished his tune on a bum note, followed a second later by a squawk from a whore who had been singing a hearty rendition of 'Dixie'.

Off to one side, Luke saw Hank Darby playing cards with a couple of other gents. Hank glanced up, raised his glass and nodded a brief acknowledgement before turning back to his game. Standing at his boss's back, Clyde grinned but it wasn't a pleasant expression.

Taking a steady breath, Luke stepped fully inside. By the time he reached the bar, a glass of whiskey was waiting.

'Drinks are on the house,' the surly barkeep said, pouring a second drink and sliding it to one side.

Luke accepted this without comment and settled on to his elbows. Around him, the room was unnaturally quiet. As he sipped the raw whiskey, watching the patrons through the mirror behind the bar, he saw Hank Darby speak a few words into Clyde's ear before the big man pushed his way across the room.

'Come to check on your odds?' Clyde asked.

He nodded to the barkeep, who pulled a slate board up from under the counter and leaned it up against the mirror on the wall behind him. Written on it were two names: Grant and Nicholls. Below them were a series of outcomes including winner, loser, one shot, two shots, and so on. Beside those and below each name were the odds.

'Two to one that Grant kills you outright. Your odds don't look too good,' Clyde mused, turning his gaze on Luke. 'Why do you think that is?'

Luke knew what Clyde's game was. There was no such thing as free board and everything on the house. Darby wanted to see what he was betting against. He had already said he didn't leave anything to chance.

'Maybe these fine betting men need a demonstration,' Clyde suggested, waving his arm around at the room. He reached into his pocket and pulled out a fistful of notes. 'I'll bet twenty dollars that Mr Nicholls here can shoot the centre out of a dime at twenty paces.'

There was a sudden flurry of activity as bets were called and money exchanged hands between men suddenly hungry for excitement.

Clyde laughed and slammed his hand down on the polished mahogany bar. 'Nah,' he said. 'Any two-bit gunslick could do that trick.'

He snapped his meaty fingers and a kid, no more than twenty years old, stepped out from the line of men standing at the bar. At first glance, he was just another cowhand with his ripped jeans, faded shirt and telltale tan line around his forehead, but with his thumbs hooked behind his shell belt and his old six-gun hanging low on his hip, he looked like he wanted to be something else. Looking into his eyes, Luke saw naïve excitement in his eyes as the kid looked him over with a smirk.

'I hear you're pretty good,' he said.

Luke stared at him.

'I'm pretty good myself. I won a hundred dollars on the plate toss at the last Fourth of July celebrations.'

'Shooting a plate ain't like shooting a man, if that's what you're contemplating,' Luke said.

'No, sir, it isn't and that's not my intention at all.' The cowhand raised his hands defensively, his attitude softening. 'But I hear Big Sam's got some old plates he won't mind getting smashed up. How about you and me step outside and set to, friendly like?'

Luke chuckled as he turned around

and rested his elbows on the bar. 'Maybe some other time.'

'You afraid Billy might beat you?' Clyde asked.

'Just thinking about you losing twenty dollars if he does.'

'Don't worry yourself. I can afford it.' He gripped Luke by the shoulder, his powerful fingers biting into flesh as he propelled him towards the street. 'Come outside where folks can get a good look at you.'

It was in his mind to tell Clyde to go to hell, but it was obvious that the big man was spoiling for a fight, and in a hand-to-hand knock-down battle Luke wouldn't stand a chance against him. The fact that Clyde was unarmed ruled out shooting him. With the crowd behind them, there was little else to do but go along. If nothing else, it would distract attention from the fact that Dan was missing and, with the hostler in plain sight, allow him and Kate to slip out of town unnoticed if Dan could persuade her to go.

Within minutes, the main thorough-fare had cleared, people moving on to the plank walks to watch the spectacle. It appeared that no one was bothered by the interruption and when Big Sam arrived carrying a stack of plates excitement was running high.

'The rules are simple,' Clyde shouted above the hubbub. 'The gun must be returned to the holster between each shot. Big Sam will throw a total of six plates into the air and whoever breaks the most wins. Billy, you'll go first.'

Playing up to the boisterous bystanders, the blond cowhand stepped forward. In steady succession six plates flew into the air, each one smashing. While Billy enjoyed his success, Luke broke the Schofield open, inserted an extra cartridge under the hammer, then slid the gun back into its holster.

'Throw!' Clyde shouted almost immediately.

Luke drew and fired, drew and fired, drew and fired, drew and fired, plates breaking left and right. As the sixth smashed to smithereens, the crowd's excitement was hushed.

'We have a tie,' Clyde announced.

In one easy movement, Luke broke open the Schofield with one hand, tipped out the spent shells, then swiftly inserted six fresh rounds. It felt easy and familiar, as did the healthy rapid beat of his heart. He held the .45 in his hand longer than he needed to. It felt good, as though it belonged there, and almost reluctantly he put it back into the holster.

'This time the rules are different,' Clyde shouted. 'Each man will face away from Sam. When I call 'throw' you'll turn and fire, then turn back again. Clear?'

Both men nodded. Luke had to admit, he was enjoying the practice — and the competition. It felt good to see faces filled with excitement instead of mistrust and loathing.

'Nicholls, you'll go first this time.'

Luke felt the silence stretch out as

Clyde paused. No doubt it was a ploy to unnerve him, but when the call came Luke spun, drew and fired in one fluid movement, shattering the plate. Again and again, Clyde tried to unsettle him, calling short and long at random, but each time the action came to Luke as naturally as breathing. Before the final fragments had settled into the dust, Luke was once again reloading.

'You ready, Billy?' Clyde asked.

As he adjusted his belt and fidgeted with the gun in its holster, it was obvious that the kid had lost some of his confidence. The small gathering also seemed more subdued. After the first shot, it was all over when the plate sailed off on to the roof of the jailhouse, breaking on impact. Before the last shot was fired, people were already wandering away, some eager to shake Luke's hand, others calling out new bets as they headed back inside the saloon.

For a change, it felt good to be Luke Nicholls.

Smoking a cheroot outside the

saloon, Hank Darby's pinched expression gave Luke more satisfaction than it should and a smile quirked the corner of his mouth. Even more so when he realized that the anger, the uncertainty that had made his heart hammer fit to explode, and the fear that had covered him in sweat, were gone.

'That was good shooting,' someone said, coming up beside him.

Turning, Luke recognized Finnegan.

'I learned from the best.'

'Yes, you did.' Finnegan glanced towards Darby, who tossed down his smoke and walked away down Main Street. 'And now he knows it. Best watch your back because Hank Darby don't like to lose.'

24

Grant refused to give Rickard the satisfaction of knowing how much the journey was taking out of him as a dull morning dragged into a dreary afternoon. It wasn't until well after midday that they made camp beside a shallow creek shadowed by cottonwoods.

'We'll wait here for a couple of hours,' Rickard announced. 'We don't want to get into town before nightfall.'

Grant was grateful for the reprieve. He had never been much of a rider, preferring to travel by stage or by train. He could hardly feel his backside and the niggling pain in his side refused to let up. After picking at a meal of cold beans and jerky, he wrapped himself in a blanket, closed his eyes and tried to blank out the inane chatter that passed for conversation between Rickard and his cronies.

As the sky darkened with the threat of more rain, he drifted in and out of sleep, vaguely aware of a coyote howling somewhere in the distance, or maybe it was a wolf: he didn't really know. The horses ground-staked nearby shifted restlessly. Opening one eye, he looked around the camp. Rickard was repacking his saddlebags, the Mexican and the weasel-faced kid were playing a game of dice. Looking further, he espied Red sitting on a boulder, rolling a smoke, with his rifle propped against his knee. As if sensing the attention, the sentry looked and jerked his head in a motion suggesting that Grant should join him.

Grant got stiffly to his feet.

'Where do you think you're going?' Rickard asked.

'I need a piss. Do you want to go with me?'

Rickard sneered and waved him away. 'Stay where Red can see you.'

Following Rickard's instructions to the letter, he walked past Red and stood a few feet beyond him. As he urinated, he turned his head and grinned sardonically at Rickard.

'You really don't like him, do you?' Red said, just above a whisper. 'How'd you get involved with him anyway?'

Grant straightened himself up and held out his hand. 'Got another cigarette?'

Red passed the one he had just finished rolling and quickly made another. He shoved it between his lips and searched his vest pocket until he found a match. After striking it twice against the boulder, it flared to life and he lit both cigarettes.

Grant took a quick draw and quickly blew out a wisp of smoke. He had never seen the attraction, but for now it offered a reason for him to linger.

'So what's the deal with you and Rickard?' Red asked.

'He thinks I owe him a thousand dollars because I cheated him at cards.'

'That's it?'

Grant shrugged. 'Why'd you call me over here?'

'I didn't want you to think I was shooting at you when this happened.'

He picked up the rifle and levered a round into the chamber. His first shot took Rickard in the chest. As the Mexican and the kid grabbed at their guns, he emptied the rifle into them.

'You're pretty handy with that,' Grant commented, looking at the bodies in the aftermath.

'It's a way to earn a living. I just made myself nine hundred dollars, plus whatever reward the railroad is offering.' Red reached into his pocket and pulled out a fistful of .45 cartridges. 'And saved you a thousand,' he said, offering them to Grant.

'What makes you think I intended to pay up?'

Grant loaded both his guns while Red circled the camp, checking on the bodies. It felt good to be free and armed again. It irked him that he hadn't been the one to kill Rickard but, in the end, the outlaw was dead and that was one face in the crowd that

Grant wouldn't have to worry about.

'Do you hear that?' he asked, inclining his ear to the west. 'Sounds like we've got company coming.'

Red grinned. 'Do you think we've got time for a cup of coffee before they get here?'

Minutes later, half a dozen armed men burst into view on the other side of the creek. Seated beside the fire, Grant didn't bother to turn and face them.

'Wondered when you'd show up, Sheriff,' Red said, holding his hand up in greeting. 'There's another cup in the pot if you want it.'

After giving instructions for the men to hold their positions, the lead rider splashed across. Despite the welcome, he approached with caution as his gaze swept the clearing and the bodies, already attracting a swarm of flies. When he was only a few feet away, he called out with authority, 'Keep your hands where I can see 'em, feller, until I get a look at you.'

'Whatever you say, Wade,' Grant

replied, turning his head.

The sheriff peered at him, gave him a good look over, then lowered his weapon and grinned.

'Bill. Heard you ran into some trouble, took a bullet. Are you all right?'

In all the excitement Grant hadn't thought about his wound, or maybe, since this wasn't the first time he had been shot, his mind had just blanked it out. Whatever the reason, somewhere along the way the pain had subsided to a dull ache. He pulled back his coat to reveal his blood-caked shirt and the makeshift bandages.

'You know me; dying ain't a priority. You took your time finding me though, didn't you?'

The sheriff climbed out of his saddle.

'Hank said you'd be headed back any day. He about blew a blood vessel when he heard Rickard had taken you off that train.'

'Doesn't sound like Hank.'

'He's been on a short fuse for a while,' Wade said, taking Grant's coffee.

'I guess he'll calm down now you're back, assuming that you're bringing him good news, of course.'

Grant's mood soured instantly. Even Wade knew it was too much to expect that the old man would just be glad to see him alive. He pushed to his feet and picked up his saddle.

'Are we standing here yacking or are we going back to town before Hank finds a reason to replace us all?'

25

At a table near the bar, Luke sipped his drink. It was only his second but he felt like he had drunk the bottle. Finnegan had joined him briefly but the big man was no drinker and had left early. He hadn't seen Hank Darby again and although Clyde had put in a brief appearance, now he was nowhere to be seen. Looking around, Luke noticed that the men who had been shadowing him were also absent.

He finished his drink and stood to leave, feeling the room tilt. When it settled he tipped his hat to the barkeep and headed back to the hotel, deciding to take in the livery, check on his horse, maybe see if Dan's grey was gone. It was past nine and although lamps had been lit along the street, he stepped uncertainly along the plank walks, using the walls for support as he crossed between buildings and empty lots.

Stopping frequently, it took him ten minutes to reach the livery stable. He had imagined it would be closed up for the night but one door was ajar and he espied a light inside. For a minute, he kept to the shadows, watching and listening. When nothing stirred, he went inside.

'Hello.'

There was no answer but when he looked into the hostler's empty living quarters he noticed a cup of coffee. It was hot to the touch.

'Hello,' he called again.

When the old man still didn't answer, he turned up the wick on the lantern hanging from a nail on the wall, then made his way along the half-dozen or so stalls. Most were empty. The swayback mare eyed him with little interest as he passed by. When he reached his own sorrel, the animal raised its head, but showed no inclination to leave. In the next stall was Dan's grey.

Luke's spirits sagged but he didn't

have time to dwell on it as the light flickered behind him.

'Are you trying to skip town?'

As he turned around, something hit him on the jaw. It was hard to say whether it was a rock or a fist, either way the result was devastating. The impact spun him around and, with arms flailing, he careered into the end of the stall. Hands grabbing him from behind stopped him crashing under the sorrel's feet as it danced to avoid him, but the outcome was little better as someone drove a hard punch into his kidneys before spinning him around for a final punch to the gut that knocked the wind out of him and brought up all the bad whiskey he had drunk.

'Son of a bitch chucked on me. I'm going to — '

'What's going on here?' someone shouted.

Despite the grogginess, Luke thought he recognized the hostler's scratchy old voice.

'Seems Mr Fancy Gunman didn't

understand Mr Darby's instructions about not leaving town. We caught him trying to take his horse.'

'Well, it looks like you boys have made your point. Perhaps you'd best leave him be now. The way I hear it, Mr Darby wouldn't like it if you killed him.'

After some grumbling, the assailant released his grip on Luke's shoulder. When the floor came up to meet him, Luke hit it hard, but it didn't matter. Right then he was too groggy to notice much except that he thought he was going to vomit again.

'You boys aren't taking him back to the hotel?' the hostler asked.

Boot soles brushed Luke's shoulder as someone stepped over him.

'He ain't dead. He can walk back by himself . . . or crawl for all I care.'

Both men chuckled as they left him there, the pain starting to hit him from several places at once.

'Do you need some help?' the hostler asked, standing over him. 'He don't look like much, but they tell me Kelly's got a punch like the kick of a horse.'

'Kelly,' Luke mumbled, determined to remember the name. 'Just l-leave me a minute.'

He wasn't sure how long it actually took him to heave himself on to his knees but the effort was wasted. When he put weight on his hand it buckled, the pain so violent that he had no control over the spasm that laid him out again. He accepted the hostler's help and, once he was on his feet, held up his hand to the light. The knuckle behind his small finger was swollen to twice its size and there was no way he could bear to move it.

'Looks like you busted your hand.'

'It'll be fine,' Luke said, knowing it was a lie. 'I just banged it when I fell.'

He left the stable with as much fortitude as he could muster, under no illusions that he was hurt bad. With his head spinning and his legs not fully communicating with his brain, he stumbled his way back along Main Street.

26

Luke had previously noticed the doctor's house that stood next to an empty lot on the edge of town. Finding out the location of the sawbones was a habit he had acquired since being shot for the first time. Before that he had never given much thought to anything but finding a saloon and a hotel, but almost dying had given him a new perspective.

Before he had finished knocking, a light appeared inside and the door opened. The doctor, a clean-cut younger man, didn't ask any questions as he helped him inside, and Luke guessed he must look as bad as he felt.

Half-carrying him along a corridor with several doors off it, the doc pushed him into a room at the far end and lowered him on to a hard upright chair.

'I have to admit,' he said, starting his examination with the lump on Luke's jaw, 'that after what I've heard around town, I wasn't expecting to see you this soon.'

'I can always come back.'

'That's not necessary,' the doc said, pushing Luke upright as he started to slouch. 'Besides, I don't think you could make it out through the door anyway. Just sit there and take it easy while I finish having a look at you. Tell me what happened.'

'A couple of men jumped me. I think my face put up a good fight but not so much my stomach.'

'At least your sense of humour is still intact.'

'Yeah.' Luke lifted his hand. 'Just tell me what you think about this.'

'How did that happen?'

'I hit it when I fell; edge of a stall, I think.'

The perpetually concerned expression deepened on the medic's pale face.

'How bad is it? Don't sugar-coat it,' said Luke.

'Pretty bad for a man in your

profession, I'd say. That lump over your knuckle, that's at least one broken bone.'

If he hadn't felt so groggy, the news probably would have panicked him, but as it was, he just sighed.

'Can you fix it?'

It was a stupid question, but in his fogged-up brain it had to be asked.

'In time for your meeting with Mr Grant? I'm sorry, no, I can't.'

Luke sighed again, feeling oddly calm and resigned. 'Grant's waited for four years. He'll probably wait another couple of weeks. Wrap it up and I'll be on my way.'

The doc frowned. 'Besides the fact that you're obviously not yourself, it's not that simple. I'm going to have to wait for that swelling to go down some and then I'll have to realign the bone.'

'How long will that take?'

'Hard to say, but I'll have another look in the morning. In the meantime, let's get you cleaned up.'

After the doctor helped him ease out

of his coat Luke hardly noticed as he ministered to his various cuts and bruises. He vaguely heard him say that there were no broken ribs, but mostly everything was just noise as he stared at his disfigured hand. It was starting to pulsate and swell more now, the redness turning into a pale but distinct bruise that spread across the back of his hand and down his fingers.

'Say, would you mind if I spend the night here?' he asked, eyeing the bed behind him.

The doc grabbed him as he swayed towards it. 'I was going to insist on it.'

'And one more thing. Have you seen the man who came into town with me?'

'You mean Dan Keen?'

The hint of familiarity in the doctor's question momentarily brought Luke alert.

'He's over at the jail,' the doc finished.

Luke tried to rise, but the doc pressed a firm hand on his shoulder.

'He's all right. The deputy's just

holding him on a false drunk and disorderly charge to make sure he doesn't leave town. He'll be released as soon as the sheriff gets back.'

'How come you know all about it?' Luke asked.

'I saw them taking him in. He had a cut on his head. It was enough for me to visit him without arousing suspicion.'

'Why would you arouse suspicion?'

'I'm a relative newcomer to Springfield.' The doc chuckled. 'They don't trust me yet. If they'd known Dan and I were old friends, I wouldn't have gotten within fifty yards of him.'

Despite the pounding in his head, Luke was curious. 'What's your name, Doc?'

'Tom Butler.'

Luke dredged his memory as the name struck a faint chord.

'You were working as a deputy in Greens Town at the same time as Dan. He wrote to me about you, said you were a good man in a fight. How come the career change?'

The doc hesitated, then replied: 'I killed a man during a bank robbery. After that, I decided I wanted to be the one saving lives, not taking them.' He picked up a bandage and started rolling in the loose end. 'You ever think of a career change?'

'Never really considered that killing men who wanted to kill me was a career.'

The doc nodded. 'That's good to know, I guess. Still, it might be something you need to think about.'

'Are you trying to scare me, Doc?'

'You told me not to sugar-coat it.' He stopped what he was doing, giving Luke his full attention. 'Mind if I ask you a question?'

Luke just wanted to lie down and sleep, forget about what had happened and hoped he woke up to find it was a bad dream but, since that didn't seem likely, he just shrugged.

'What are you going to do when Grant shows up?'

'Why, did you put some money on

me?' Luke chortled, although he didn't really know why.

'I don't gamble. If I did, I wouldn't gamble on a man's life,' the doctor said stiffly. 'Dan told me you intend to go through with Hank Darby's proposal.'

'You know about that?'

'Whole town knows about it. Half of them are ready to pack up and leave if Grant takes over.'

'Good job nothing's changed, then.'

'You mean you're still planning on a showdown with him? Isn't that going to be nigh-on impossible to win now?'

The doctor's scepticism didn't surprise him and for some reason he felt inclined to dispel it, albeit cryptically. 'Let me ask you a question,' he said. 'If you came across a man in the middle of nowhere, shot to hell, and you didn't have any of your medical supplies with you, what would you do? Walk away?'

Butler physically recoiled at the suggestion. 'Of course not! I'd do what I could to save him with what I could find.'

'Well, there's your answer.'

The doctor looked confused but Luke didn't feel like elaborating. Then someone banging on the door stalled any further questions. Luke glanced at the clock hanging on the wall behind the doc's neatly ordered desk. It was just past nine.

'Bit late for visitors, isn't it?'

'It's not unheard of.'

Even so, Luke felt there had been enough surprises for one evening. As he followed the doctor into the hallway, he reached around with his left hand to pull out the Schofield. As Butler opened the door, Luke leant back against the wall and waited.

'You're wanted over at the house.'

'What's happened?' the doctor asked.

'Got a man with a bullet wound needs your attention.'

Luke recognized Clyde's oafish voice and, slipping the Schofield into his belt, he stepped into view. 'When did Grant get into town?'

'Didn't say he had.' Clyde's eyes

narrowed. 'What are you doing here?'

'I had an accident.'

As the doctor stepped aside to collect his bag from a side table, Clyde got a better view of his injuries and a grin split his angry visage. 'Jesus! The boys said they'd had a bit of fun with you. What's wrong with your hand?'

'Busted. Be a few weeks before I can use it . . . assuming I live that long,' he added with a smirk.

The doctor turned a frown on him.

'Was it Kelly that did it?' Clyde asked. 'Curly-headed kid?'

'Does it matter?'

Clyde looked unsure how to answer, which seemed out of character, but it made no difference to Luke. Right now he needed to get some sleep, if he *could* sleep with his head pounding. With Grant back in town, he was going to need his wits about him. After a nod to the doctor, he walked away without looking back.

★ ★ ★

214

Sleep hadn't come easily to Luke, but he woke with the first grey light of dawn, his nose twitching as the aroma of coffee and the sound of Tom Butler talking to someone drifted into the sick room. Reluctantly, he eased himself into a sitting position and pulled on his boots, tuning his ear to the conversation taking place somewhere along the hallway.

'I thought Grant was going to kill him,' Tom said. 'You know how big Clyde is, he must have eighteen inches on Grant, but the big man was scared. When Grant drew one of those Colts and shoved the muzzle up under his chin, I thought he was going to pee his pants.'

'I'd be willing to bet he wouldn't be the first.'

Luke recognized Dan's voice.

'Clyde was real careful when he told his story,' Tom went on. 'Made it clear he'd had nothing to do with it.'

'And how did Grant take the news?' Luke asked, wandering into the small kitchen where both men were seated at the table.

He noted the neatly stitched gash that had split his friend's right eyebrow, the dark circles under his eyes, and the worry etched in the deep lines on his forehead. Apart from that and the need of a razor, he appeared none the worse for wear.

They, in turn, looked him over. Tom had probably seen worse and looked to be making an assessment. Dan's expression was more revealing. Luke hadn't given much thought to how he must look, but if Dan's empathetic wince was anything to go by, it couldn't be good.

'Mad as a wet cat,' Tom said.

'You're lucky he didn't turn on you,' Luke opined, helping himself to coffee from a pot on the stove.

'He did but Hank Darby reined him in, said he might need me.'

'Speaking of which, how bad was he shot?'

Tom considered his answer.

'Let's just say, it won't slow him down any.' He got to his feet, assuming a more professional air. 'How are you feeling?'

'Like a herd of buffalo ran over me — twice.'

'Your hand?'

'I don't think I'll be playing the piano for a while.'

'Shall we find out?' Tom didn't wait for an answer as he pushed past. 'I'll be in the treatment room when you're ready.'

Luke held back.

'Is there anything I can do?' Dan asked.

'Make sure Kate knows Grant's in town,' Luke told him. 'You and I both know he won't forget about what she did to him. Tell her what's happened to me and be sure she understands how serious the situation is.'

Dan sucked in his breath. 'Do you?'

Luke grinned despite the pain lancing through his jaw. 'Neither of us bakes cookies for a living. You worry about yourself and let me do what Ben trained me for.'

27

A couple of hours later, with his hand supported in a sling across his chest, Luke arrived back at the hotel. The clerk smiled uneasily as he handed over Luke's room key. Several guests on their way out stepped aside as he passed them on the stairs. When he reached his room, he placed his ear close to the door before opening up and pausing on the threshold to look around.

Nothing appeared to be out of place. The bed was made, the furniture was straight and there was clean water in a pitcher on the dresser. Spying his image in the mirror on the wall, he realized why folks had been making way for him. The colour had drained from his face, serving to highlight the vivid purple bruise that accentuated his swollen jaw. The heavy bandage that extended up his sleeve, keeping his broken bones in place, left no doubt that he was badly injured. It sure hurt like hell.

Refusing to dwell on it, he moved to the wardrobe and swung open the doors. Taking out his saddlebags, he carried them to the bed, unbuckled the strap and took out the oilskin. Looking at it, he knew someone had been there, searching for the Schofield no doubt; a quick glance on the floor quickly located the thin strip of leather that had bound the package.

He unwrapped the contents and stared at the old leather belt holster. It was empty, of course, and he smiled as he reached round to the small of his back and pulled the missing gun from the waist of his pants. Deftly, he unbuckled his rig, added the holster, then buckled the belt back round his waist. Finally, he broke open Ben's Schofield, checked that the chambers were empty, then slipped it into the holster on his left side.

He would have liked to clean and oil it, but it would have been impossible to do that one-handed, so for the next few minutes he concentrated only on the gun, letting his hand find its position, his fingers brushing the handle. Gradually he increased the movement, lifting the weapon from the holster then dropping it back. It had been a long time, but he remembered the feel of it. Again and again he repeated the exercise, each repetition smoother than the last.

A knock sounded at the door, bringing him up short.

'Who is it?'

'It's Dan.' He entered without waiting, pulling up as he eyed the gun aimed at his middle. 'Can I come in or are you going to shoot me?'

Luke lowered the Schofield. 'It's not loaded.'

Dan strode to the windows, twitching the curtains as he looked down into the street. 'Better put six in then because Grant's heading this way and he looks like he means business.'

The news wasn't unexpected. Grant was nothing if not predictable. He lived his life like some character out of the pages of a dime novel.

Luke sat down, cracked open Ben's Schofield and wedged it between his knees. Steadily, he loaded cartridges into all six chambers, aware of Dan staring at him.

'What happened when you spoke to Kate?' he asked, deflecting whatever Dan was itching to say.

'It shook her up. She wouldn't leave town, but she agreed to stay at Tom's until this is over.'

'Good thinking.'

'I was hoping you'd see it that way. Tom's handy in a fight. She'll be safe there. It's time you start thinking about yourself.'

'Not quite. You and me need to get a couple of things straight first.'

'Such as?' Dan scowled.

'You being a lawman, for starters. This thing between Grant and me ain't your business. It's time for you to walk away.'

'Strictly speaking, Grant made it my business when he kidnapped a woman in my town. Even if he hadn't, I wouldn't leave now.'

Luke shifted his arm in the sling, sighing as he considered his throbbing hand. 'You know this doesn't make any difference, especially now I've got this.' He hefted the Schofield on his palm. 'It feels like being reunited with an old friend.'

'This is still Darby's town and Grant is Darby's man.'

Luke shrugged. The facts didn't make any difference to him. Wherever he went he was an outsider, but he knew what Dan was driving at. Chances were that whatever the outcome between him and Grant, he was a dead man.

As if jumping from his thoughts, Grant's voice reached him from the street.

'Nicholls! Get out here. There's something you need to see.'

28

Luke was almost glad of the interruption. It didn't pay to dwell on things that were beyond his control and allowing doubts to creep in would get him killed as sure as day followed night. Looking out of the window, he saw Grant standing on the plank walk opposite. Kelly was with him, a wide grin spread across his face as both men looked up at the front of the hotel.

'What the hell?' Dan asked.

Luke opened the windows, keeping to one side.

'What do you want, Grant?'

With folks already scattering and the street falling into an ominous silence, it was a moot question.

'Step outside. There's something I want you to see.'

Luke's gaze scanned the street, his mind starting to reason. He saw no sign of Hank Darby among the crowd of onlookers and it seemed unlikely that Grant would force a showdown without him present, the older man having gone to such great lengths to get Luke there.

Whatever Grant had in mind, Luke doubted he would put himself at a disadvantage by giving Luke the high ground.

Dan grabbed his arm. 'You're not going out there?'

It sounded more like a fact than a question but it didn't change anything.

'If he was here to kill me he'd call me down on to the street.' Luke dropped the Schofield into the empty holster and tugged at the edges of his coat. They refused to meet over the bulkiness of the guns and he let them fall apart. 'He wouldn't risk letting me have the higher ground.'

Dan picked up the Winchester that had been leaning against the wash-stand.

'I hope you're right, but whatever happens, I'm behind you.'

A cool breeze wafted against his face as Luke swung open the tall windows. Weathered boards creaked under his boots as he stepped out on to the narrow balcony that ran the length of the building and led to a set of steps at the end.

Even from way across the street, he saw Grant's dark gaze taking in every detail, his eyes narrowing as he tried to ascertain whether Luke was carrying a gun. Beside him stood Kelly, whose grin widened.

'You look like hell,' he shouted. 'What happened to your hand?'

'I broke it when you bushwhacked me. Doc says it could be five or six weeks before I can use it.'

Kelly laughed and turned to Grant.

'Did you hear that, Mr Grant? Seems like I done you a favour. Mr Fancy Gunman's as harmless as a dead wasp now.'

Grant's gloved fist smashed him in the face, the force propelling him halfway across the street, where he lost his footing in a wheel rut and landed on his backside.

'What was that for?' he grumbled, stumbling to his feet and slapping dried dung off his pants.

'For thinking I needed your help.' Grant peeled off his left glove and flicked back the edge of his coat, leaving his hand poised near the Colt. 'Draw.'

Kelly backed away.

'I ain't got no beef with you, Mr Grant.'

'Draw.'

'I didn't mean no harm,' Kelly whined, his head swivelling towards Luke. 'Tell him it was an accident.'

Luke shrugged.

'I said, draw.'

Kelly's hand moved to cover the pistol carried in a holster on his loose-hanging belt. 'You should have seen him. He was real fast. Real fast. So sure of hisself, he needed taking down a peg. I just wanted to — '

'Draw, you stupid son of a bitch!'

Panic-stricken, Kelly snatched for his

gun, but Grant didn't move as he fumbled it from the holster. Luke almost felt sorry for the man as he saw a naïve smile touch his quivering lips. He really seemed to believe he had a chance but, as he brought the old six-gun up and reached to cock it with his other hand, the roar of gunfire rent the silence.

Kelly's innards exploded out of his back as at least a couple of bullets found their target, and with smoke still curling from the muzzle of Grant's Colt, Kelly's mangled body hit the hard-packed earth with a dull thud.

'Anyone else in this godforsaken town feel like interfering in my business?' Grant shouted. Casting his gaze around the onlookers, he emptied out spent casings and reloaded the Colt.

29

The silence marked a stark contrast to the excitement that had surrounded the expectation of a showdown. It seemed that in the cold light of day, the reality of men dying was too horrific. But as they looked on, their expressions a mix of shock and fear, Luke doubted anyone would readily admit to betting against Grant.

'I'd say they got the message,' Luke called without shifting his position. Grant stepped off the plank walk. 'Is it true you can't use that hand?'

'Yep.'

'Seems a mite convenient. Are you sure you ain't faking?'

'You don't have to take my word for it.' Luke nodded along the street. 'The doc's coming along right now. Why don't you ask him?'

'Maybe I would if I gave a damn.'

Grant rammed the Colt into its holster and pulled on his glove. 'But the way I see it, it's your concern not mine.'

The threat barely raised Luke's pulse. 'So it was never about a fair fight then?'

'A fair fight?' Grant asked. 'I almost killed you once and I wasn't even serious about it back then.'

'Maybe the incentive wasn't big enough.'

Grant took a pace forward, lip curled in an ugly snarl. Gone was the look of manic excitement that usually accompanied his threats. Now his obsidian eyes burned with unfettered hatred, his natural arrogance replaced with murderous intent. It took Luke by surprise and his left hand moved towards his waist.

'Do you think I care about money?' Grant growled.

'I wouldn't know what makes a man like you tick.'

Grant went noticeably rigid and, like the hand of a clock clicking on to change the hour, the familiar crazed look came over him.

'Gratitude.'

Luke raised an eyebrow.

'Gratitude to the man who saved a whore's bastard from a life of ridicule and hardship, taught him how to shoot and how to hate, showed him that respect isn't earned, it's taken.'

Luke sniggered. 'Sounds like a lot of hard work to me.' Grant shook his head.

'Not killing you, that's been hard work. Making sure you didn't swing from the end of a rope for killing that woman, that was hard work . . . and expensive. Do you know how much it costs to bribe a judge and jury? Close to a thousand dollars.'

Luke's stomach flipped. 'You're saying you were the reason I went to jail instead of swinging from the end of a rope?'

'Funny, ain't it? And that's not even the best part.' Grant's eyes bulged with glee. 'It was me that killed Lucy Johnson.'

'Much as I'd like to believe you, the truth is it could have been a stray bullet fired by either of us.'

'No. It was mine. I made sure she died.'

It was unbelievable but Luke had to ask. 'Why?'

'Because she meant something to you.'

'I didn't even know her.'

'It didn't look that way to me. That charade in the street — her dropping a can, you picking it up for her — it didn't fool me. The look on your face when she touched your arm, told me everything I needed to know.'

Luke shook his head in disbelief. It had been a chance meeting, no more than a minute. No one in his right mind would have given it a second thought.

But Grant was never in his right mind.

Luke's fingers curled around the Schofield. His first shot hit the dirt where Grant had been. Luke ducked low, running along the balcony as shots peppered the wall behind him. He barely managed to stay on his feet as he hurtled down the steps and into the alley at the side of the hotel. A few strides brought him level with the street, where he pulled up and waited as people ran past, panic-stricken and desperate to escape the line of fire.

Within minutes, the street lapsed into silence. Luke broke open the Schofield, careful not to eject the unspent rounds, and replaced the empty shell. He peered around the corner and quickly spotted Grant hunkered down behind a horse trough a hundred yards away.

'Are you ready to end this, Grant?' he shouted.

'I was born ready but you know we can't start without Hank. He's waited a long time to see this.'

'Forget Hank. He missed his own brother's death — do you think he's gonna worry about yours?'

30

Kate stood with her back against the door where she had been since Tom Butler had left minutes earlier wearing a gunbelt and carrying a rifle. She had seen his indecision when the first gunshots had echoed along the street, the hesitation as he went to the dresser in the hallway and retrieved the weapons. On his way out, he had reached for his black medical bag, pulling his hand back at the last moment.

Even now she was tempted to grab it and run after him. Racked with indecision, she jumped as a fist pounded against the door.

'You in there, Doc?'

Someone tried the handle; the key rattled in the lock as pressure was applied against the heavy wooden panels.

'Leave it, Clyde,' someone said, struggling through a fit of coughing. 'He probably heard the shots, same as we did.'

'Should I check the back, just in case?'

'Don't bother. When this is over there'll probably be more need of an undertaker than a doctor.'

Someone chuckled, then the sound of footsteps faded as they left.

Kate made up her mind. She grabbed the bag. Even as she forced shaky hands to unlock the door, more sounds of gunfire reached her ears. Within seconds she was out on the street, just a few hundred yards from the action. Ahead of her, two men were walking into the middle of it.

She ran for the cover of the general store, pressing herself flat against the wall and inching her way towards the voices. Over the pounding of her heart she thought she heard Luke.

'Forget Hank. He missed his own brother's death — do you think he's gonna worry about yours?'

She gripped the bag tighter against her and ran on, aware of several people watching her as she passed the barber's. The next lot was empty and she hesitated, teetering on the edge of the plank walk as the distinctive sound of a rifle being cocked echoed between the buildings. It had seemed to come from across the street and, looking up, she saw a man on the roof of the bank, about to shoot. As her eyes followed his aim, she glimpsed Luke throw himself backwards a split second before a bullet hit the wall inches above where his head had been. As her gaze spun back to the shooter, blood drenched his chest before he could pull the trigger again, the rifle clattering on to the plank walk below.

She looked back to where she had last seen Luke, but he was out of sight. A movement on the balcony at the front of the hotel caught her eye and she spotted Dan Keen, working the lever of the Winchester. Even before he fired, gunfire crashed from several different locations. As she threw herself down, she caught sight of Tom Butler standing between the jail and the bank, a rifle drawn up to his shoulder as he levered and fired in quick succession.

Behind him the bank's plate-glass window shattered and someone inside screamed. Butler turned, then staggered and fell, blood staining the back of his shirt as someone fired from the jailhouse.

'Hold your fire! Hold your goddamn fire!'

Kate realized the order had come from one of the two men she had been following, the one who was fighting for every breath as he almost coughed himself off his feet. Amazingly, he was standing in the middle of the street, undaunted and unscathed. More surprising still was the fact that the shooting died away to nothing as quickly as it had started.

★   ★   ★

His back pressed against the wall, Luke reloaded as he waited to hear what Hank Darby had to say.

'You boys just hold it a minute,' he called, his gaze switching between them. 'I brought you here to do this properly.'

'Keep out of this, Hank,' Grant warned him. 'This is between me and Nicholls.'

'The hell it is! I've waited too long to get you two together and finish what Ben and me started.' Hank leaned against Clyde's arm, seeking support as he struggled against a fit of coughing. 'You denied Ben the right to see it through, but you won't ruin it for me.'

'Get lost, old man. This ain't about you and your brother any more. Step off the street unless you want to join Ben sooner than you planned.'

'You might want to think that through,' Hank wheezed, 'before you do something you won't live to regret.'

Again the sound of rifles being primed echoed along the street.

'What the hell, Hank?' Grant shouted.

Hank chuckled. 'You seem to forget, William, this is my town. I give the orders here, not you. Either you play by my rules or you die by them.' Standing level with the alley, he turned to face Luke. 'Same goes for you, Mr Nicholls.'

'And what are the rules?' Luke asked.

'You and William will face each other and when I give the word you'll both draw and fire until one of you is dead.' Hank's watery eyes rested on the twin Schofields for a few seconds. 'I see you have Ben's gun after all. It's good to see them back together one last time. Are you as good as he was?'

Luke shrugged. 'And when the smoke clears, if I'm still standing, do your men have orders to gun me down?'

Hank shook his head. 'I stand by the original terms of the agreement. Winner takes all.'

'And if Grant tries to change the rules and shoots me dead the second I show my face on the street?'

Hank grinned and looked up towards the hotel balcony. 'I'm sure your friend up there will shoot him dead. Then my men will shoot your friend dead.'

'A win-win for you.' Luke dropped the Schofield into its holster, resting his hand on the butt. 'Let's get this over with, then.'

Luke wondered how many of Hank's men were left. He had seen a few fall when the shooting started and there were none in view as he took a quick glance and stepped on to the street. He didn't recognize the look on Grant's face. As his gaze flicked between Luke and the rooftops along the street, he looked almost amused.

When they were about thirty-five feet apart, Hank called for a halt. Supported by Clyde, looking decidedly uneasy, he walked to a point midway between them and took a few steps back.

'Ready?' he asked.

'Hey, Nicholls, do you think you'll get a shot off?' Grant shouted.

Luke adjusted his arm in the sling,

then dropped his left hand to hover over the Schofield.

Grant laughed, baring his teeth like a sick dog. 'It's a shame what happened to your hand. I guess that after I kill you, some people might say it wasn't a fair fight.' He sucked in his breath and made a show of giving the idea some consideration. 'I could let you draw first, give you a chance.'

'Call it,' Luke said, without taking his eyes off the man he had come to kill.

'Good luck, gentlemen, and may the best man win.'

Luke's hand dropped on to the Schofield.

'Draw.'

Grant's right gun cleared leather as Luke's fingers gripped the Schofield and started to pull it clear of the holster. He had never noticed it before, but Grant pulled high, turning his shoulder before he fired. It took a split second and it allowed Luke to shoot from the waist. His shot hit Grant in the hand, smashing it and causing the

241

gun to spin away in a spray of blood.

As Grant grabbed his mangled fingers Luke's second bullet took him in the upper arm. Almost as if the shot had surprised him, Grant faced Luke and two more shots pounded into his torso. He staggered and fell, remained unmoving in a puddle of his own blood.

Hank lurched towards the body, his legs barely seeming to hold him up. 'You killed him.'

Luke's gaze scanned the surrounding buildings, alert for any movement, any sign that Hank intended to renege on the deal. Above the saloon a curtain fluttered in an open window, further afield a dog started barking, doors creaked and whispers mingled with the lingering gun smoke. From the balcony of the hotel, Dan watched the rooftops, his glance meeting Luke's briefly, a slight nod acknowledging his relief.

'Is it over?' Luke asked, seeing Hank back away from the body.

Hank reeled, his eyes refusing to focus as he turned his pale, ravaged face on Luke. Stooped and grasping at Clyde's arm for support, he coughed globs of blood into the dirt. In the space of a minute, he appeared to have aged ten years.

'Yes,' he managed to splutter. 'It's over. Ben won.'

31

After the echoes of gunshots faded away, an eerie silence hung over Main Street. As Kate watched the smoke clear, it seemed like the whole town was waiting for something else to happen. Somewhere a dog barked, breaking the spell, a signal that life must go on. Within minutes, people began to filter out of the surrounding buildings. Kate moved along with them, stumbling towards the scene.

'Is he really dead?' she asked.

Standing over the mangled corpse, Luke prodded it with his toe. The blood-soaked body rocked like a piece of meat. Grant, the man who had killed her husband, was gone and what remained was only a shell.

Kate had expected to feel a sense of justice. All she really felt was disappointment and a sense of guilt. Frank was still dead and Grant had never relented. She hadn't pulled the trigger that ended his life, but she had wanted him dead and knowing that she had sunk to his level of violence left her cold, numb.

'You must be Ben's wife,' the coughing man said. 'I'm sorry we're meeting in these circumstances. I'm Hank, Ben's brother.'

He extended his hand but she ignored it, keeping her eyes turned away from him, too sickened to look him in the face. 'Did you order Grant to kill him, to kill your own brother?'

'Ben's stubbornness got him killed. If he had just stuck to the agreement . . . '

She held up her hand, refusing to listen to his pathetic excuses. 'I don't want to know.'

'It wasn't personal,' he added.

For the first time, Kate took a good look at Hank Darby. She felt slightly queasy. Seeing Hank was like seeing a ghost, in more ways than one. Pale, gaunt and weak, using the giant beside him for support, Hank was a sick man. When he hacked into his handkerchief, she noticed the blood soaking through it and on to his fingers. It was a sign she recognized. Her father had died from consumption. She had nursed him until finally it took him. If her guess was right, Hank Darby was nearing the same miserable end.

The knowledge stirred mixed emotions, tempering the animosity that she had felt towards him.

'We should get to know each other,' he said, as if they were meeting in pleasant circumstances. 'Ben would have wanted me to make sure you were taken care of.'

'I'm sure he wouldn't,' she said with cool certainly.

After all, she hadn't known Ben Darby. Didn't want to. There was nothing to be gained from learning the truth about a man who had chosen to hide his past from her while he was alive. It was a shame for Hank though. True, her husband had lived with regrets that kept him awake at night and drove him to the bottom of a bottle during the day, but there were things she could have told him about Frank. How he abhorred violence. How he yearned to settle down and start a family. It still hurt her knowing that's was what had got him killed. But none of that mattered now.

'You never knew my husband,' she said, turning away as an unexpected swell of emotion caught in her throat. 'His name was Frank Portillo and he was a good man.'

⋆　⋆　⋆

Luke fell in beside her as she walked away, unsure whether she would want his company now that she'd had her revenge. She had shown loyalty to her husband and a lot of dignity, but she had also expressed contempt for the kind of man he was — the kind of man Luke was.

As they reached the bank, Tom Butler

staggered out, supported by a fat man in a suit and a woman in a flowery bonnet. His complexion was almost grey, his shirt sodden with blood, but he smiled and nodded. Luke pressed in beside him, taking his weight from the woman. Kate did likewise, elbowing the fat man aside despite his protests. Dan joined them as they reached the doc's house, and together they managed to patch him up.

Later as they sat drinking coffee in the kitchen, Dan asked, 'What will you do now?'

Luke thought about it, his eyes wandering to Kate, who had said very little. Although the swelling had gone down around her nose and eyes, the evidence of Grant's handiwork still marred her pretty face. Her hair hung in limp tangles around her slumped shoulders. It saddened him.

'Someone suggested I might change my name, make a fresh start,' he said.

'Sounds like a wise man,' Dan opined.

'What do you think, Kate?' Luke asked. 'Is it a good idea?'

She looked up, met his gaze with a flat stare. 'It won't be easy. Not with those guns hanging round your waist.'

He unbuckled his belt and handed it to Dan.

'What about now? Do I look like the kind of man you'd want as a . . . friend?'

She stared at him, a small glint coming into her eyes.

'I'm not looking for a friend any more — and you told me once before that you're not the marrying kind.'

'I wasn't, but a man can change, can't he?'

Dan got to his feet. 'I think I should look in on Tom, let you two talk awhile.'

They waited for him to leave.

'There's something you should know before you decide,' Kate said. 'I'm carrying Frank's child. That's what got him killed. He didn't know it; thought I was just sick. That's why Grant caught up with us. Frank had a rule, never stay

249

in one place too long. He broke it for me.'

The news was both elating and saddening, but Luke sensed there was more to the confession.

'Why are you telling me this now?'

She chewed her lip. 'He was your friend; can you forgive me?'

It was a lot to take in but nothing that needed much thought. He had only known her for a few days and already he couldn't imagine never again seeing the twinkle in her blue-green eyes or the smile on her lips. That she was carrying Ben's child, Ben's true legacy, was more than he could have wished for.

He got up and walked around the table, drawing her up against him. 'Do you blame yourself?'

'No.'

'Then there's nothing to forgive.'

He pressed his lips against hers.

She didn't try to stop him.

He was glad about that.

Other titles in the
Linford Western Library:

A DARK DAWN IN TEXAS

Richard Smith

On her deathbed in the spring of 1875, Laura Peters shocks her son Paul by belatedly revealing that his uncle did not die alongside his father in the bloody confrontation at Gettysburg twelve years before. She urges Paul to ride west in a quest to find this relative who holds a guilty secret from those dreadful Civil War days. With mixed emotions he takes up the challenge, eventually arriving in the Texas town of Ongar Ridge — only to find himself accused of murdering the man he has been seeking . . .

DAYS OF DUST AND HEAT

Walton Young

During the hot summer of 1888, three men are travelling by train to Cheyenne. Luke Tisdale, a medical doctor, seeks to claim the body of his murdered brother and find his killer. Marcus Stokesbury, a newspaper reporter from Atlanta, is in pursuit of a story about the mysterious third man, Ezra McPherson. Haunted by a violent past, Ezra becomes caught up in the conflict between the Wyoming cattle barons and homesteaders. He faces a stark choice: either run from the imminent range war, or enter the field of battle . . .

LONG RIDER

Colin Bainbridge

Wes Stretton has ridden a long way to gain vengeance on Yoakum, whom he holds responsible for killing his friend. The trail takes him to the town of Buckstrap, where he meets the enigmatic Lana Flushing and walks straight into a range war between rival ranches, the Bar Seven and the Sawtooth. Someone knows of his arrival, however, and is out to bushwhack him. Then the foreman of the Sawtooth is shot. But was Stretton the intended target? And is Yoakum the culprit — or are things not quite what they seem?

BLOOD FEUD

Bill Grant

When Montana prospector Luke Driscoll receives a letter from his estranged brother Nate urgently asking for help, he returns to his home in Garrison, Texas. There he learns that Nate has become embroiled in a land dispute with cattle baron Robert McTavish — and it's about to turn deadly. But Luke also meets the lovely Miranda, McTavish's eldest daughter, and cannot help his feelings for her. Now Luke must balance family loyalty and his budding love for Miranda to fight the determined and resourceful McTavish and his crew of hired killers.

THE DARK TRAIL TO NOWHERE

Harry Jay Thorn

Lucas Santana is a freelance range detective — and a wanted man in some states — who has several aliases; nor is he shy about lining his own pockets in order to finance his Wyoming ranch. When a number of gold coins surface in South Texas, loot from a big heist years back, both Pinkerton and the US Marshals call on his services to find their source. Problem is, Santana's not the only one searching for it — and when a fellow agent is murdered in cold blood, his quest becomes personal . . .